A DOCTOR IN EXILE

When Doctor Leonard Bordon went to Columbia as part of a United Nations team to determine the need for hospitals, he had no idea that he would stay two years instead of one, or that he would find the most lovely woman he had never seen and would marry her. Nor did he know that he would end up in the distant, little-known and insular village of Puna in the Magdalena Valley, but all these things happened—and more.

The rich landowner Jorge Ritter Avila opposed both progress and Doctor Bordon until a gunshot laid him low, and the Indians as well as local mestizos were sullen towards Eloise Cutler, the beautiful head-nurse at the Puna dispensary. On top of that there was the misery, the anguish, the intolerable ignorance. Leonard Bordon had to overcome all of it and he did, but it was no easy undertaking. But Doctor Bordon was no ordinary doctor.

A Doctor in Exile

by
MARGARET STUART

ROBERT HALE · LONDON

© *Robert Hale Limited 1968*
First published in Great Britain 1968
Reprinted 1980

ISBN 0 7091 0047 7

Robert Hale Limited
Clerkenwell House
Clerkenwell Green
London, EC1

Printed and bound in Great Britain by
REDWOOD BURN LIMITED
Trowbridge & Esher

Chapter One

There is a steep, winding mountain road, hair-raising still after hundreds of years, which is the lifeline of Bogotá, Columbia. Over it are hauled raw materials, industrial machinery, replacement parts, oil, food, all the needs of an industrial community which chance put at a rarefied altitude and which stubbornness has kept there.

All around is the Cordillera, the giant snowcaps, saw-toothed ridges, twists and bends, dark canyons and wind-scoured plateaux which typify Columbia. Uninitiated lowlanders round the world think of Columbia in Latin America as one of those steamy, humid banana republics. It isn't. There is rarely a month that passes when frost doesn't whiten the highlands. People with bronchial or heart trouble can die in that altitude without a sound.

But Columbia is a hurrying little place. Its progressives want to push it bodily into the twentieth century. Its liberals insist that the United States and other industrialized countries help with great infusions of capital. Its conservatives, on the other hand, want foreigners to keep out. They want liberals declared outlaws and Communists, synonymous under their privately sponsored laws, and they want the progressives to either be quiet or at the least, to join with them in bringing progress to the country in

5

such a manner that the conservatives can and will control it.

The Magdalena Valley lies at an elevation of nine thousand feet above sea level. The Bogotá road drops down into it near the Magdalena River, a brawling cataract of very cold water. Near the summit, before the swift descent is made, stands one of those small, weathered shrines to be found throughout South America where lorry drivers pause to light a candle and breathe a quick prayer, either for having been allowed to reach this point without accident, or to plead for safe passage on the downward journey to the lowlands beyond the Cordillera.

They usually make it. Not always, but usually. Because the road is so rough, so narrow and pocked with such futile guard-rails, when someone drives over he never survives. The drop is awesome. Below, there are jagged rocks waiting.

When Leonard Bordon initially made the trip he alternately sat petrified, and cursed himself for ever agreeing to come to this windy, desolate, poverty-ridden place. His Indian driver was, unlike most Indians in automobiles, a sane, calculating, very calm individual. He took few chances, drove carefully, and pointed out to Dr Bordon where the year before his good friend Sancho Avila had been lost over the side, and also, nearer the little shrine, where one Pablo Echavarria had either lost his brakes or his steering mechanism, and had also been smeared over the rocks so far below.

Dr Bordon had agreed to come out to the village of Puna to make a preliminary examination of the residents of Magdalena Valley to determine, for the Columbian Institute of Agrarian Reform (INCORA), whether a hospital was warranted.

He'd only reached Bogotá a week earlier from London *via* New York, and it was not an easy transition at best, but now, looking down the crinkled bonnet of the old car into the valley below, he felt more than ever convinced he needed his head examined.

There were a thousand ways for a man to die. In civilized lands at least five hundred of them had been eliminated. In Colombia none of them had; even if he survived the road, reached his allotted village of Puna and successfully completed his task, he'd still be subject, just as were the natives, to every single one of those illnesses, accidents, or biological failures. *Providing* he first survived the trip into Magdalena Valley. At the moment, poised like a martyr in the ancient car with his impassive mestizo-Indian driver, he had no guarantee he'd survive at all.

He asked if the brakes would hold for the road seemingly dropped away beneath them. The Indian solemnly inclined his head. He spoke English; in fact he spoke it rather well. But he remained an Indian. Fatalism was fine in its place. Leonard Bordon just didn't believe *he* had any right in that place.

'You see where the rock walls come closest down there on both sides of the river, Doctor?' A very dark, roughened hand pointed. 'There was once a railroad trestle there.'

Dr Bordon, gazing at what was left—little enough —and kept waiting for the tale of what had happened to the trestle and the railroad. He was never told.

And that was another thing that frustrated him. Both mestizos and Indians had the most infuriating habit of making a simple statement, then never elaborating upon it as though, since, for example, that trestle was no longer operative, there was no point in discussing *why* it wasn't.

The old car shuddered, eased over and began the descent. His driver's only comment was a laconic one to the effect that while normally he'd most certainly have lit a candle at the Madonna's little shrine back there, because he'd neglected to bring any candles this trip he'd be unable to. But, since he'd driven this road hundreds of times, it was more than likely they'd reach the valley without difficulty.

It was by then early afternoon. By the time Leonard Bordon caught his first sight of Puna in its inhospitable, barren setting of volcanic rock and flinty soil, a blood-red sun whose normal golden rays had to be first filtered through layers of wind-scourged dust, showed up as a miserable collection of hovels, several earthen streets, several stores and a number of electric poles unsteadily supporting swinging, slack power lines.

He thought that if he'd closed his eyes and had tried to imagine the least inviting, most squalid, backward and ignorance-steeped village on earth, he couldn't have dreamed up anything quite so appallingly ugly and repelling as the town below. Even that reddish sunlight across corrugated iron roofs didn't make it look picturesque.

The driver, whose name was Narcisso Pinzon, came out of his stoic calm once, where the steepness abated a bit, turned, studied Leonard Bordon's bronzed, tough and youthful features, then softly said, watching the road again, 'I tell you something, Doctor. My country is very poor, as you've seen. Even Bogotá with all its fine buildings and great plazas is poor. But here, in the Cordillera, there is poorness such as you may never before have seen. So I tell you something: The people are touchy about their backwardness. You must understand.'

Dr Bordon looked at the dark, coarse profile. He was being given some off-the-cuff advice. It was being offered gently and in good spirit. He looked back towards the road, willing to listen.

'Maybe they told you in Bogotá that my country is going to do great things. I too have listened to those rich men speak like that. But I tell you something, Doctor, it will be a long while coming, all this greatness. Meanwhile, don't compare us with where you come from. Don't find fault, because the people will be expecting you to do that. Don't give them any reason to hate you—because that's what they're waiting to do.' The very swarthy unattractive face swung to show a sad smile in muddy dark eyes. 'I want you to succeed down there.'

'Why, may I ask?'

'Well,' said Narcisso Pinzon, 'I am a peasant. But I have been many places. Once even to Tampa in Florida. I learned English as a common seaman. I know —because I have seen it—how backward we are. But *I* couldn't make these people believe it and I am one of them. For you—they will hate you if you even try. So, I want you to succeed down here because you are their hope. And my hope too, Doctor, because you and I know something *they* don't know. *We* know you can help them very much. *We* know how terribly they need that help. Only *they* don't know it.' The coarse, thick-featured face was unsmiling. 'I can't say it right. I know that. But I *feel* it and I want you to also feel it. You are a good man, Doctor. I've seen others before you. I think you are the best they've ever sent out.'

A Doctor in Exile

Leonard sat thoughtfully turning this speech over in his mind. He knew one thing; these people could actually *feel,* sense, instinctively grasp, much more than one normally would imagine possible. It was part of their mystique, and it also happened to be factually true.

'Thank you,' he finally said, as the road began levelling off. 'That's probably the best advice I've received since arriving in Columbia, Narcisso. I'll certainly remember it.'

The black Indian was patently pleased. All the rest of the way down he sat with a little soft smile holding up the corners of his fleshy lips. Then, when he could resume normal driving range, he said, 'The lady I brought in to boss the native nurses last month ... Well ... she is young. . .'

Leonard understood what it was Narcisso Pinzon wanted to say but didn't know how to put it. He said, 'I see. She hasn't worked out very well, eh?'

'Oh, she works out very well, Doctor. She works hard, knows her trade ... But she ... People can *feel* when someone hesitates to touch them. They know what that look in her eyes is—Dirt. They are dirt to her.'

'And they hate her, Narcisso?'

'Well, give them another month. They will burn down the dispensary. They will do everything they can to break her heart, her spirit. They will spit at her when she walks past. They will revile her in Spanish and Quechua. I tell you something: I drove her down here exactly as I'm driving you down. I knew how it was going to be for her.'

'Did you try to advise her as you've done with me?'

The coarse head with its mane of straight black hair

10

wagged from side to side. 'Doctor, there are some you can talk to, some you can't.'

'I see.'

'Doctor, I tell you something: I don't want that dispensary burned. I don't want her run out. I'll take two candles back up the mountain with me on the return trip. One to be sure I'll make it through the mountains again, as I always do, the other for you. I won't be back at Puna for ten days. I'll pray that when I come back with your boxes and medicines you will have got that lady straightened out like she should be.'

Dr Bordon, seeing the road on ahead both flat and level, loosened all his muscles and nerves which had been taut for so long, leaned his back back and closed his eyes.

God what a fool a man became when he gets carried away by illogical compassion. Not only was he being dropped into a place as remote and alien as the moon, but his only trained and reliable assistant was turning out to be some kind of female bigot!

Chapter Two

Inside a stone-fenced pasture horses grazed on brush and very little else. Cows wandered thin and listless, among the earthen houses and the thin garden patches. There were also mules, sad, suffering animals with clouds of egg-laying flies massing round the raw sores on their backs where packsaddles without pads had dug holes in the flesh.

But the town was actually pleasant. It looked anything but pleasant from above, but as Leonard Bordon reflected, perhaps the road up there coloured the first view.

Dark children tumbled out open doorways and came running from behind homes and stores at sound of Narcisso Pinson's old car. They'd have done the same for *any* car because, although cars did arrive in Puna rather frequently—at least once or twice a week—they were nonetheless interesting for what they brought. Puna's lifeline was the Cordillera road; all blessings as well as curses, came down that road in automobiles.

Older people, more inhibited, came to stand in doorways and look, dark, impassive, still as stone, quiet as the night. Incas: descendants of a vanquished greatness.

There was a plaza. There was *always* a plaza. One of the most charming aspects of the Spanish tradition is the plaza. Here, in the plazas of Latin America, have rung the *gritos*, the calls to rebellion against cruel tyranny. Here all momentous pronouncements are made. Here too, doe-eyed maidens are eyed by young bachelors. Here are the buildings of the officials, the *mayór*, the jailhouse of mud with walls three feet thick, the constabulary barracks—of wood, incidentally—and most of the shops and stores.

There too was the INCORA office and off a few buildings was the hospital—actually a dispensary since it had nothing but three small examination rooms, one long ward of iron cots and a dingy reception room.

There was also a baroque building, incongruously topped by a modern corrugated iron roof, complete with sentry-boxes on each side of a tiled-over grand gateway. This was the dilapidated hotel. It had obviously been the manor of some proud dignitary of the Spanish Empire a hundred and fifty years earlier. Only the dark genius of its impressed Indian artisans had insured that it should still stand for clearly very little had ever been done to maintain the building.

There was the church, of course; no Columbian town is without the epic structure of dominant catholicism. There would be a priest. In places like Puna he would not, in all probability, be eloquent nor very light-skinned; those eloquent priests would be kept in the larger cities. Leonard Bordon didn't know this, but then he'd never been in Latin America before.

There was a soldier, complete with ugly little sub-machine gun slung from his shoulder, dressed in olive green fatigue uniform, smoking a cigarette and watching the jeep from in front of the jailhouse. He was

13

squat, evil-looking, pock-marked and very tough in appearance.

'Well,' sighed Narcisso Pinzon, leaning over his steering-wheel. 'Welcome to Puna, Dr Bordon.' He grinned showing large, even, very white strong teeth. 'You weren't so sure we'd make it, eh?'

Leonard didn't return the smile. 'I hoped, Narcisso, I hoped.'

The Indian laughed, heaved his bulk around and alighted. Several men ambled over, stony-faced but willing to help carry the doctor's boxes and bags into the dispensary. They said nothing and Narcisso did not offer to introduce any of them. There was no rudeness to any of this, nor any oversight. This was how everyone except Dr Bordon expected the thing to be done.

One man caught and held Dr Bordon's attention. Primarily because of his size. Mostly, the Indians were average in height or slightly less than average. This man must have been well over six feet tall and correspondingly wide and thick. He had a machete in its scabbard at his side. His khaki shirt was open to expose part of a bronze, powerful chest. He had a beard, which was unusual. It was close-cropped and very black. The man stood apart and no one looked at him although patently everyone around was conscious of his presence. The man definitely was unfriendly. Leonard could sense that across an intervening distance of perhaps two hundred feet of plaza roadway.

The dispensary was clean, smelt of disinfectants, and someone had tried valiantly to change the mouldy interior of the place but without very much success. Two small Indian women in white, starched dresses came forward to offer shy and uncertain smiles. They said in passable English that *Hermana Eloise*—Sister Eloise—was busy with a patient and would be along as soon as she'd finished, meanwhile they'd show the doctor where his office would be.

Narcisso Pinzon went along, a thickly made, stoic man with muddy black eyes which missed nothing, but who had nothing to say. Later, he helped Dr Bordon get settled in the small office, furnished with two steel filing cabinets, a battered table and two old chairs. When they were alone, Narcisso stood a moment gazing out a window. 'It is a poor place, you see,' he said quietly, and slowly turned to watch Leonard drop into one of the chairs. 'It will be a test, Doctor.'

'A challenge,' contradicted Dr Bordon, and smiled. 'Narcisso, do you know what makes someone accept such a challenge?'

'No, *Señor*.'

'You. People like you who have some idea what must be done—must be overcome. People who have faith in someone else's capacity.'

The black eyes brightened, the doubt vanished. 'Then you will do it. Doctor, I think I must be about forty years old. And I have seen many things in those years. I tell you something: Even an Indian learns after a while to know other men. When I first took you into my car in Bogotá, I felt you were exactly the man for Puna. If you want to know—I have faith in you. Well, now I have to start back. It's not a good thing, getting caught up there in the clouds after nightfall. But I will be back next week with your other boxes.' Narcisso thought a moment then said, 'There is Father Lopez at the cathedral. He will help.'

Narcisso departed and Leonard Bordon sat a while

in the reddish afternoon gazing out the window Pinzon had stood by. In the blurry distance were mountains as high as any he'd ever seen before. Nearer lay hovels and muted noise and dusty earth. It was hard to imagine why there was a town here at all, except that perhaps in Viceregal times this valley had perhaps been strategic.

One of the little dark nurses timidly knocked and entered. She said she had been instructed by Sister Eloise to go arrange for rooms at the hotel for Dr Bordon, and if he would give her the money she would go at once.

He arose, stretched, said he'd take care of that himself, thanked the nurse and ambled back out into the thin warmth of dying day.

Across the road the stocky soldier in high boots, rumpled green fatigues and shoulder-slung submachine gun stoically eyed him. He walked on over.

The soldier straightened a little, drooped his smoke and waited, unsmiling. He wasn't very old, perhaps twenty-two or three. His eyes were cruel, hard, and almost scornful, but his lips showed contradicting lines made by laughter.

Dr Bordon said, 'Good evening.'

'Good evening, Doctor.'

Leonard thought word certainly travelled fast, and said, 'Do you have political prisoners in the jailhouse that you guard it with a gun?'

The soldier shrugged. 'Just prisoners, Doctor.' He plainly wasn't certain whether his wards should be classified as political prisoners or not.

'May I see them?'

The soldier shrugged again, turned and unlocked the door, kicked it open and a powerful stench came forth. Inside, there was an unlit dank corridor with three cells, all quite large, like animal cages, on the right side. On the left side were two individual cages with an office between them. These were empty but the large cages held perhaps a dozen people each. One prisoner was a girl of perhaps sixteen or seventeen suckling a scrawny little child with watery eyes and limbs like matchsticks. It was, in Dr Bordon's eyes, a scene shockingly like something from Dante.

The prisoners, mostly men, looked dully out. The child-mother didn't even bother to raise her head from the baby. Leonard turned to the soldier. 'What has the girl done?'

'Prostitute,' he said without interest.

'And the baby?'

The soldier looked blank.

'The baby can't have committed a crime.'

The soldier understood. 'Oh. Well no, but he is in here.'

'How did he come here?'

'How, Doctor? Why, he came in with his mother.'

'And these others?'

'Cattle,' said the soldier in soft Spanish, looking at the mute and motionless older prisoners. 'Theft, mostly, but also they are suspected of being guerillas or at least of helping the guerillas.'

'How long have they been here?'

'Well, I have only been here two months. They were here when I arrived.'

Leonard returned to the roadway, breathed of the fresher air and waited until the soldier had locked his door again. There was a hurrying figure coming up the centre of the plaza roadway, the only person thus far Dr Bordon had seen who wore a necktie.

'Doctor,' the newcomer croaked as he almost ran forward. 'Dr Bordon I am Elfego Sanchez, the mayor. Why do you go into the jailhouse; you should have come for permission to me first.'

Leonard gravely shook the mayor's hand and eyed him. Elfego Sanchez was wizened, thin, nervous, obviously educated as well as vociferous.

'The soldier here let me see inside,' he told Sanchez. 'Why is the girl kept in that hole with all those men, Mayor Sanchez?'

'Why not, Doctor? If I release her she will go get diseased again.'

'She could be found a suitable job couldn't she?'

Sanchez said, 'No, *Señor*. She has been set free before. Come, walk to my office with me.' Leonard nodded to the soldier and turned away. As they walked Elfego Sanchez explained. 'At least in the jailhouse the girl is fed three times a day. Her child is safe. If I set her free she would lose the child—he would die of pneumonia because, having no place to stay, she would have to take him around with her at night while she went about her trade.'

They halted outside a whitewashed mud building next to the baroque hotel. It was Mayor Sanchez's office. They were looking southward down across the plaza towards the towering mountains Leonard Bordon had just traversed. There were lowering, dirty clouds among the peaks.

'What of the other prisoners?' asked Bordon.

'The military has charge of them. They've been bringing in people like that for a long while. Since the last serious trouble.' Mayor Sanchez pointed towards a building with trees shading it. 'That is our school, Doctor. There have been no classes held there

18

for six years.' Sanchez dropped his arm. 'Twenty years ago we had a bad outbreak here. The army came with tanks, airplanes, automatic weapons. The *bandoleros*—which is what they call peasants in revolt—were decimated. Captured ones were brought to the school yard. Men, youths, women, children, old people.' Sanchez groped for a limp handkerchief to mop his face. Returning it to a pocket he said, 'Well, they tried a few and executed them. Then one day a truck drove up to the playground, all the prisoners were marched out, two machine-guns were set up and they killed all of them.'

Leonard felt a coldness in his heart. He stood staring at the school building with its blessed tree-shade and benign shadows.

'Twenty-five hundred of them,' concluded Mayor Sanchez. 'Some did not die immediately. They were then bayoneted.'

It was a bad moment. The doctor stood there in his red-shaded alien world ringed round by immense mountains, aware of the brutality in human nature, listening to the talk of a man who did not, obviously, approve, yet who could understand such a pig-sticking, which meant that to him it was part of the warp of human existence.

Children darted among the stores shouting at one another. People strolled the plaza with the swift, soft patter of their language rippling across the evening to where Leonard and Elfego Sanchez stood. A soldier emerged from the yonder barracks picking his teeth. An old man, bent and crippled in the joints, made his slow-painful way into the dispensary where now a light was shining.

Weariness hit Dr Bordon like a physical blow. It

had been a long day. He excused himself and went to the hotel, arranged for a room and went up to it.

There was a bed, a single electric bulb hanging from the ceiling, a pair of ancient curtains over a window overlooking the plaza, and a smell of mustiness. He had no trouble at all imagining how this building had formerly rung with the contemptuous ribaldry of Spaniards—and he could understand exactly what it was in the Indian nature that had made the Spaniards take that view of their 'animals'.

Chapter Three

Father Eusebio Lopez was a dark, crew-cut young man, very earnest, educated and willing. His cathedral was old, neglected, and when Dr Bordon visited it, quite empty.

Eusebio Lopez wasn't more than perhaps twenty-five years of age; possibly thirty but no older. He struck Leonard Bordon as a collegian. He was muscular, clear-eyed, with an inquiring expression and a soft little spontaneous smile. He of course knew who Leonard Bordon was and introduced himself by his name, not his title. 'Eusebio Lopez,' he said. Not 'Father Lopez.' Leonard got the impression from that, that Lopez was perhaps new in his tonsure and robe.

As they strolled through the church, Father Lopez explained some of the history of his cathedral. Surprisingly enough, it wasn't a particularly bloody nor exciting history. Currently, said Father Lopez, it had also served as a hospital during the occasional skirmishes between *campesinos*—peasants—and constabulary soldiers.

'Not that they don't all know of the hospital,' he added quickly, 'but you must understand that when these people think they will die they prefer to do it in the church.'

Leonard nodded. He was not a Catholic, hadn't been raised in an atmosphere compatible to catholicism, knew nothing about it, really, but was a fair, open-minded man so he listened, and when he could get in a word as they emerged upon a long, gloomy outside corridor running the full length of the rear of the old building, he said:

'What have the uprisings meant, Father, in terms of practical existence?'

They sat on a big oak bench. Father Lopez said, 'In terms of practical existence, Doctor, is the only way they mean anything at all, for the church has failed here, as elsewhere. It's not enough to salvage the mestizo or Indian soul but that's mostly what the church has concerned itself with—not with the belly. The uprisings. *Señor*, have to do with hopelessness, with hunger, with hardship you wouldn't believe. For land, *Señor*. The Institute of Agrarian Reform will come to parcel out the land. You have come first to care for the ill. Well, Doctor, that is political, is it not?'

'Political? Father, I'm a medical man.'

'Of course. But before the government can make these hopeless people listen it must first demonstrate its sincerity. So you come; Miss Eloise Cutler comes; some teams of surveyors, agronomists, even a veterinarian, came. Carefully at first, and slowly. After all, this is a troubled province, Doctor, and anyway these people have been scratching in the rocks for centuries, so another year isn't likely to make much difference.'

Leonard settled back. This was straight talk from a knowledgeable young man. 'Go on,' he prompted.

'The church has been content too long to let things stand as they are and always have been. My predecessor told me they would come and kneel and beg us to help them. He said we should of course pray for their damned souls but otherwise the church's business has

22

nothing to do with people such as George Ritter Avila.'

'Who is he, Father?'

'Yesterday when you arrived, do you recall seeing a big bearded man with a machete in his belt? That was George Ritter Avila. He heads the large land owners. He has vowed war if INCORA attempts to parcel out the land. He is wealthy and very strong in the uplands. He is no mean enemy, Doctor, and he is now *your* enemy. He is also my enemy, but he laughs at me, makes his telephone calls to Bogotá, and I get a telephone call back telling me to celebrate more Masses, to concern myself more with salvation, less with politics.'

'And you obey,' said Leonard, studying the toes of his shoes.

'No, Doctor, I do not obey. I hold more Masses and I try to give hope. But I also speak for freedom, for dignity, for at least some small advance towards equality.'

'Do they listen to you, Father?'

Father Lopez candidly shook his head. 'No. But as I said, the church has failed them. Come next Sunday —half the church will be empty. No young people come at all. They have told me—'Father; perhaps you mean well, but so have others and we still starve. We do not believe guns are best, we only know they are surer and we will no longer await your miracles." So, Doctor— welcome to Puna.'

Leonard raised his eyes to catch the expression of soft irony. He smiled. He was a head taller than Father Lopez. 'Thanks, it's nice to be welcomed. After my visit to the jailhouse last evening and my talk with Mayor Sanchez, I expected an older, fatter priest.

Lethargy, Father, is another name of arterio-sclerosis of the brain.' He arose. Sister Eloise, as everyone called Eloise Cutler, had sent word she'd be in his office at noon today. As they strolled back through the gloomy, high-ceilinged old church, their footsteps sounding like sand dropping in an hour-glass, Leonard said, 'Tell me about Mayor Sanchez. Do the people have faith in him? They must to have voted him into office.'

'He wasn't voted into office, he was appointed by the military governor.'

Leonard let his breath out slowly. An iron band was tightening around his heart. This was all like something one read about; dictatorship in the guise of democracy.

'But Elfego is not a bad man. He is not strong, nor perhaps very wise, but he dislikes much that goes on, only what can he do?'

'He might *try,* Father.'

Eusebio Lopez's youthful, bright eyes lifted. 'Doctor, judge none of us until you've been here at least six months.'

Leonard did not say he was only supposed to stay two months, determine the health of the natives, how many people were likely to need medical assistance, then report back to Bogotá. He didn't say any of this because, beginning with Narcisso Pinzon, he'd got a firm impression that these people were depending very much on him—or on *someone*—who might come to save and help them.

It was not a position he delighted being in. In fact, thinking back to the conferences back in Bogotá with international officials, INCORA representatives, even Columbian civil servants, he could not recall a single

24

one of them hinting that what he might find in Magdalena Valley would be as things actually were.

Of course, probably like Father Lopez's predecessor at the Catholic church in Puna, he was supposed to narrowly follow the guidelines set down; was to look, to examine, observe the need, should one exist, for a proper hospital, then simply return to report as much.

As he strolled over to the dispensary he had some difficulty adjusting to the barrage of new thoughts. He was no crusader, at least in neither the political nor social sense. In his homeland-world he belonged to a system which, while perhaps imperfect, was nonetheless orderly, organized and equitable. He'd read of distant places but he'd never before actually seen emaciated babies in prison cages, nor seen the hopelessness in human eyes he'd seen in Puna in only two days of being there.

He entered the dispensary, saw a row of silent people lift black eyes at his presence, nodded a little self-consciously, and went on through to his little office.

It had been dusted, his books placed on a shelf, his pen-set put in the middle of the rickety table, and the window had been opened to let in fragrant summertime warm air.

'Satisfactory?'

He turned. She was tall for a girl, perhaps five feet six inches. Her eyes were violet, her hair, close-cropped, curly, was ash-blonde. She was extremely lovely. He was astonished for he'd imagined something different. Eloise Cutler had a beautiful figure. In fact, Eloise Cutler *was* beautiful.

'Quite satisfactory,' he said, and smiled. 'Please come in Miss Cutler.'

25

She closed the door at her back, discreetly glanced at her wristwatch—making certain he saw her do it —and stood waiting like a soldier.

He moved a chair. 'Please be seated.' She obeyed, but still like a soldier. He was of course used to discipline and some formality but this was overdoing it. He perched on the edge of the old table until it ominously creaked, then went round to the chair and sat behind the table gazing at her.

She had the full, ripe red lips of a girl but with a slight tightness at the corners. Her gaze was direct and assessing. She was taking his measure even as he was taking hers.

'You are busy, of course,' he murmured, 'so I won't detain you very long.' He looked at his hands. This really wasn't a job for a physician. 'Well, as everyone seems to know I'm Leonard Bordon. I'm here to make a survey for the hospital board. That's about all I have to say, except that perhaps I can help in the dispensary.'

Her nostrils fluttered. That was the only movement he could detect before she spoke. 'You can help, Doctor. This isn't a place for a nurse. What is needed here is someone who can remove cataracts, diagnose intestinal ailments, treat glaucoma, make the officials *do* something except stand around wringing their hands and sympathizing.'

The words had come like bullets. The voice had been soft, yet harsh. Eloise Cutler was sitting erectly, even indignantly, across from him, her eyes bitter, her lovely mouth pulled flat.

'Of course,' he said, and leaned back thinking of Mayor Sanchez and the armed soldier over in front of the jailhouse. 'But first let's try some social medicine.

26

Have you ever seen the inside of their jailhouse?'

'No.'

'There is a girl over there whom I'd guess to be six-teen years old. She has a baby I should say is six or eight months old but it looks to be a month old.'

'Malnutrition is common here, Doctor.'

'All right. But let's bring them over to the dispensary.'

Eloise Cutler looked resigned. Leonard thought it was because he was bringing another patient, but the moment he remonstrated, she set him straight.

'I don't object to the girl. Perhaps she'll have enough sense to become an aide, although they usually are too stolid and withdrawn, but if she doesn't speak English it will be difficult. However, that's not the point, Doctor. Why don't you go see Mayor Sanchez first, before becoming gallant?'

Leonard nodded a trifle grimly. 'I see. You don't believe they will release her.'

'I don't know the girl, Doctor, so I can't be sure, but I *do* know something of Puna, and you don't.'

'I'm listening, Miss Cutler.'

'Have any of them told you about a man named Jorge Avila?' Because she gave the first name its Spanish pronunciation he almost shook his head.

'George Ritter Avila, Miss Cutler?'

'Yes. I see you've heard of him. Well, the next time Elfego Sanchez is wringing his hands and rolling up his eyes, denouncing the viciousness of their rural system, laugh in his face. I think your girl, along with all the others locked in the jailhouse, was brought here by soldiers led to her hiding place or her mud hovel by Jorge Avila.'

27

'You think, Miss Cutler . . .?'

'I've already said I know nothing of the girl. But I *do* know how the others got here because I saw the Avila truck bring them in. She was probably among them.' Miss Cutler arose, standing very stiff. 'I'm sorry, Doctor, but we have a heavy load today. It is Saturday.'

He also arose. She'd mentioned it being Saturday as though that were important. He could have enquired but he didn't. He said, 'I'll go with you.'

She started to turn doorward, then stopped to consider him. Her voice softened slightly, her hard eyes assumed a detached expression. 'You've read books on European debtor prisons of the Middle Ages, I'm sure. Well, we try to be cleaner but we don't always succeed. I have two day nurses and one night nurse. We usually have anywhere from ten to thirty in the beds. I am allowed no funds for charwomen, so if the dispensary doesn't measure up, Doctor, please understand why.'

He waited for her to finish. He was a patient, even-tempered man but she'd irritated him since she'd stepped into his office. 'Do you suppose people who volunteer to come to these places expect perfect schedules, immaculate dispensaries and ideal conditions? I'd rather thought a volunteer would want to come so he could establish those things. I did. I hope you also did.'

He started towards the door to hold it open so she could pass through first. He was thinking of the look on Narcisso Pinzon's face.

A church bell pealed. Instead of sounding clear and sharp-cut in the Cordillera's thin, winey air, it sounded mournful. Or maybe that was just his own gloomy reflections making it sound like that.

Chapter Four

The cases were no more than Leonard Bordon had expected. Except for a broken leg—the gift, so the patient said, of his mule for all the excellent care the man had given the ungrateful, wretched beast. Thinking of the sores on the backs of mules he'd seen, Leonard had reservations.

There was a woman in labour. She thinly smiled up at him from her iron cot. She knew only one English word, evidently—'thanks'—which she used quietly, then used her own Spanish word to describe her situation. '*Episodio*'.

Leonard smiled. He liked her sardonic toughness. He knew a little Spanish—actually not very much although he'd been given a 'crash-course' before being sent to Latin America. To the woman this was her 'episode'. She doubtless had many other children. This was her *episodio*, rather like spring fever, being here each summer to be delivered of a child.

There was a swaggering, fiercely moustached, very flat-faced mestizo whom the other people tried studiously to ignore. He'd suffered a serious fall from his horse but was ambulatory now and would shortly be discharged. Eloise said in a lowered voice: 'One of Jorge Avila's cowboys.'

She didn't say any more but then she didn't have to. Leonard smiled the man indicating a chair. 'I'd like to examine your head, please.'

The *gaucho* gave Leonard a long, scornful look then motioned '*Hermana* Eloise look—not you.'

Eloise turned pithy. 'He is the doctor, Alfredo. He will examine you.'

Alfredo curled his lip contemptuously. 'He don't do nothin' to me. Only you, *querida*.'

Leonard understood the word of endearment, reached, caught tight hold of Alfredo, forced him into the chair and still holding him by the shoulder in an iron grip, said, 'I do the examining. You keep your mouth closed until I'm through.'

Alfredo, perhaps more astonished than anything else, blackly blinked, but he also obeyed. Afterwards, as he arose, someone in a distant bed whistled. It was the high, steady whistle used by Latin Americans to indicate derision. Alfredo whirled but it was impossible to determine who'd done that. He swung back. Leonard stood squarely in front of him, waiting.

Alfredo started to say something but there was a look on Dr Bordon's face that silenced him. Eloise Cutler waited until the bad moment was past, then she turned to take Leonard among the other patients. Up near the far end of the dingy room she finally tapped his arm and said, 'Doctor, it's not the wisest thing to antagonize Avila's men.'

He nodded and stepped beside the nearby bed to lean and look into the hopeless, listless eyes of a very old man.

There was nothing wrong with the old man, or perhaps everything was wrong with him. He had to be at least eighty, his eyes were milked over by cataracts, his skin was dryly cracked and weathered to a dark

30

chocolate colour.

'The eyes,' said Eloise Cutler. 'He could still see a little when his family brought him here to die, but since then. . .'

Leonard made a minute examination. When he straightened up the old man hadn't moved so much as a finger. He was. perhaps off wandering in some shadowy byway of his distant youth.

'We'll remove the cataracts,' Leonard said.

Eloise looked shocked. 'Where? With what instruments?'

'Right here if we have to, and I brought adequate instruments. What's the matter, Miss Cutler? An hour ago you were villifying Mayor Sanchez, the system, everything within sight for dragging heels. Now it's you doing the dragging.'

He left her in the ward, strolled out to the front reception centre where the two little dark nurses were briskly at work speaking Spanish among the patients out there—mostly women, young and old. A few got past to be admitted to the ward but the majority got simple cursory examinations, some salve or pills and were sent about their affairs. It was of course a very unorthodox routine and yet it was evidently satisfactory. Besides, he mused walking over where a wooden file cabinet stood, this was Magdalena Valley, Columbia.

There was a rather good set of records at the dispensary, all hand-written in neat, artistic script. Miss Cutler's, no doubt. He decided to begin compiling the statistics he'd need the following day and strolled outside to stand a moment in pleasant golden sunshine.

Mayor Sanchez was walking along with a roll of papers under one arm looking morose. The moment he saw Leonard he veered over, brought out the rolled up papers, opened them with a flourish and held the first one up. All Leonard could make of the Spanish wording was something to do with land reform. He nodded encouragingly. It was the wrong expression.

Sanchez rolled his bundle up again, said a tart curse and pointed. There was a neat, narrow, rather elongated hole through all the posters. 'The land owners,' he said bitterly, 'sent me these back. I had them posted up in the countryside for everyone who wants to participate to see, then come down here and fill out the forms. Each family is to get twelve and one-half acres.' He rolled his eyes. 'None will come. That machete thrust through the posters is an even more compelling directive, Doctor.'

Leonard took a long chance. Perhaps it wasn't so long after all, but at least he'd seen no one else sporting one of those big knives. 'Avila?'

Mayor Sanchez looked sharply upwards. 'Who can say? *Some* land-owner of course.'

'Aren't they to be paid rather well for the land taken?'

'Yes. *I* think so and doubtless, since you've been told they are to be paid, you also think so. But—*they* don't think so.' Sanchez paused, frowned, then said, 'Well, perhaps they don't object so much to the payment as to the government forcing them to tell unused land. It is communistic, they say, and they will resist.'

Leonard stood there studying Mayor Sanchez. What odd manner of chameleon was this man? If Miss Cutler was correct, then Elfego Sanchez belonged to Avila, yet here he stood with his torn posters looking forlorn and deeply upset. Sanchez solved the dilemma very neatly without any prompting.

'Doctor, we are both professional men. I am secure in my office as long as this *departmento* is peaceful. Do you understand? This is a very unpleasant position to be in.'

Leonard almost smiled. Elfego Sanchez probably had the best-paying, most prestigious job of his entire career. He might belong to Avila, but privately he was strictly the man of Elfego Sanchez!

A man rode round a corner on a large reddish horse. Sanchez, with his back to the newcomer, did not see him. Leonard recognized the man at once. George Ritter Avila. He was curious about the large man. In some ways Avila was quite mestizo, in other ways he seemed European, or at least partly European.

The horseman saw them standing out front of the dispensary and reined over. Elfego Sanchez looked, gave a small start and said, *'Señor! Buenas dias!'* He acted thoroughly delighted, as though Avila were a long-lost brother.

The large man ignored Sanchez to stare from gold-flecked light brown eyes at Leonard. Up close it was obvious Avila was indeed more European than Columbian, although he was enough of the latter to be a native. The close-cropped black beard made him look evilly Spanish. His size did the rest. It was no wonder the natives dreaded him. Leonard had to adjust just to the man's obvious antagonism without considering his size.

The tawny eyes shifted. 'I see you got the posters back,' said Avila, in a strangely gentle, pleasantly deep voice. *'Señor* Sanchez—no more.'

Poor Sanchez stood and perspired. Fortunately this little interlude where he was being humiliated was only witnessed by Leonard Bordon, which obviously was exactly what Avila'd had in mind.

'I have said it before—no posters, no surveyors on my land, none of those other people on any of the estates.'

'But *Señor*,' protested poor Elfego Sanchez. 'It is the law. I am told what I must do. It's not *me*—it is the law. I must put up the posters and. . .'

'They can't read them, *Mayor*. You know that.'

'Perhaps not, but the law says I must put them. . .'

'No more,' roared the large man straightening in the saddle and swinging his tawny glare. 'Dr Bordon, I am Jorge Ritter Avila.'

Leonard nodded without uttering a sound. It was improbable Avila negated him to. It was also noticeable that Ritter-Avila negated the European blood he carried. Every word, look, action, was entirely Latin, entirely Columbian.

'We don't need a hospital here, Dr Bordon. The clinic is enough. We need nothing here. Least of all we need land reform; people like yourself, foreigners and troublemakers here. Doctor, the sooner you finish your work and leave, the better.'

Avila reined around and rode off at a jog. The horse had a load but he was equal to it. Also, he was a sleek, well-fed, very powerful animal, in sharp contrast to the *campesino's* animals, chewed raw, wormy, sick and lustreless.

Leonard watched Avila ride away then turned his attention to Sanchez. The mayor was mopping sweat again. It wasn't that warm, moreover they were standing in shade.

Miss Cutler stuck her head out. 'Doctor, I have a person I'd like you to look at.'

He excused himself, nodded to Elfego Sanchez and followed Miss Cutler inside. She took him almost to the ward doorway then she stopped and turned.

'You have now met the formidable Jorge Ritter Avila. What was your impression?'

'Ethnically? I'd say German and Spanish.'

'Not ethnically, Doctor. You know what I meant.'

He grinned at the stern but very lovely visage. 'Disagreeable, discourteous, troublesome—and large enough to eat hay. Well, lead on, let's see this patient.'

'There is no patient.'

He looked at her. 'Then why are we playing charades, Nurse?'

'Avila's cowboy Alfredo, climbed out a window and left.'

'What of it; he's got a skull of pure bone. He didn't have to hang about the dispensary anyway.'

'Perhaps not, Doctor. But now, with Jorge Avila in Puna, Alfredo will seek him out and make up a preposterous tale of the way you mistreated him during the examination this morning.'

Leonard was beginning to understand. 'I see, Miss Cutler, and now you're certain Ritter-Avila will come marching in here like Attila seeking satisfaction from me.'

The beautiful eyes got round. 'Doctor, this man is no one to unduly antagonize. He has already. . .'

'Miss Cutler I *do* wish you'd make up your mind. One minute you want me to sally forth and straighten out all the iniquities of this ancient system. The next moment you're afraid I'll be eaten alive.'

He turned walking briskly towards his office. He could feel her watching his progress. Also, he was

thinking of something Narcisso Pinzon had told him
—the natives did not like Miss Eloise Cutler.

He thought he understood why.

He'd brought a few of the more commonly required
drugs and medicines with him to Puna. The real
reserve, however, was back in Bogotá awaiting Narcisso
Pinzon. What he had he set about stacking on shelves.
He also set up the very small but dust-proof glass cabinet
he'd brought along, then placed his meagre assortment
of surgical instruments in the little cabinet. After that,
he went through a steel filing cabinet, found that someone the previous year had begun making a statistical
estimate exactly as he was supposed to do. It was
incomplete and there appeared to be errors in addition,
but the list was fairly comprehensive. All he'd have
to do would be to bring it up to date from the wooden
cabinet out in the reception room, revise all of it to
the current year, and he'd have his work finished.

Someone knocked timidly. He called for them to
come in and set aside the papers. He only caught a
glimpse of the frightened little nurse then she was
blocked from view by the great body of Jorge Avila.
The landowner had a braided rawhide quirt dangling
from one wrist. Evidently this was some kind of
indoor substitute for the machete, which did not
adorn Avila.

Leonard's heart missed a beat. He knew Avila was
filling that doorway to overawe him. In fact, Avila was
a very imposing figure, standing wide-legged like that,
but Leonard said quietly:

'*Señor* Avila, please come in. You'll have to excuse
my Spanish, it's pretty horrible. But you speak fine
English. Please have a chair.'

Avila entered, kicked the door closed behind himself, walked without a word to the edge of the table and fastened those gold-flecked brown eyes upon Leonard without making a sound.

Chapter Five

When Leonard had stood about as much of the intimidation as he felt he had to, he went round behind his table, sat down and gave Avila stare for stare.

'If you want to play games, go find some children,' he told the big man. 'I have work to do, so either get on with whatever brought you here or get out.'

Avila's eyes hardened towards Dr Bordon. 'Get out, Doctor? Who will put me out—you?'

'If necessary, Mr Avila.'

'You believe you could do that, Doctor?'

'Mr Avila I know damned well I can do it!'

They continued the staring for another moment, then George Ritter Avila went to that chair he'd been offered and sat. 'Well, Doctor, when I saw you getting out of Pinzon's old car I thought we would probably have a bad meeting someday.' Avila paused, looked around, looked Leonard up and down then settled back in his chair. 'Alfredo told me things he overheard here, Doctor. He also told me how he was abused.'

'You don't believe those lies, Mr Avila,' said Leonard evenly.

'No?'

'No. Of course if you're looking for some reason to be my enemy, then you'll profess to believe them. Otherwise you'll know perfectly well Alfredo is a liar.'

'He would cut your heart out for calling him that, Doctor.'

'No, he wouldn't. But he's welcome to come try if he'd like.'

Avila put his head slightly to one side. He was evidently having some difficulty coming to a firm assessment of Leonard Bordon. He didn't fear him in the least, and right at the moment Leonard didn't believe Avila actually disliked him. It was simply that he couldn't quite grasp whatever it was that represented Leonard Bordon.

'Tell me,' he finally said, 'what you are going to say when you return to Bogotá?'

'Mr Avila, I've only been in Puna two days. I hardly know what to think.'

'Then I'll tell you what to think, Doctor: We don't want any hospital here.'

'It will cost you nothing. The plan is supported by international. . .'

'We don't need it. We don't want it!'

'Who is we, Mr Avila?'

'All of us. The growers, the *campesinos*, the townfolk.'

'Are you the mayor, the governor, the judge; how do you know what is wanted here, Mr Avila?'

The big man shot to his feet, patience exhausted. He gripped the shot-loaded quirt. 'You admit you know nothing after only two days. Doctor, I've lived here all my life. I can tell you what is needed and what is wanted. That does *not* include you, or your hospital built and maintained with Communist money!'

Leonard remained seated. He studied the rather handsome but sinister face of the large man. 'I'd like to do some guessing concerning you if I may, Mr Avila.' He didn't await for the big man to acquiesce. 'You may have been born and reared here as you say, but you've been to other places in the world. Your English, for instance, is very good; you have no accent to speak of. Also, you are one of the landed class who mean to destroy everything if need be to keep your land.' Leonard leaned forward, his voice turning earnest. 'Listen, Avila, you are an intelligent man. More intelligent than the people in this village. You know damned well what'll happen to you and people like you if all these peasants are permitted to go hungry. You've already had bloodshed here.'

'We will have more bloodshed, Doctor, and I think you had better not be here when it comes.'

'Aren't you going to be paid for the land the government takes?'

'That's not the point, Doctor; if one government can decree a man's land away and pay him for it, what will stop the next government from taking away all the land he has left without paying? What is to prevent the third government from perhaps shooting a land-owner, or exiling him, or flinging him into prison for the rest of his life?'

The tawny eyes flashed steady fire. Leonard listened, nodded slightly and said, 'Governments are elected, Mr Avila. If you keep people poor and hungry they will vote against everything you stand for. Going around with a machete and a whip only confirms them in their opposition. Or do you land-owners think you can frighten the entire populace into submission?'

Avila stood as he'd stood before, wide-legged, erect and massive. He stared at Leonard for a long moment before saying, 'Doctor, in this part of the world gold talks. You say people elect governments; Doctor, you have a lot to learn.'

'Are you telling me they *don't* elect governments?'

'No Doctor. What I'm telling you that while the people *do* elect the governments, it is landowner-gold that buys them afterwards.'

Leonard went to the office door when someone knocked briskly. It was Eloise Cutler. She didn't act the least bit surprised to see Avila in the office which meant that little frightened nurse had rushed to tell her.

She said, ignoring the big man, 'Doctor, if you were serious about removing the old man's cataracts, he will be ready in fifteen minutes.'

He thanked her, closed the door and said, 'Mr Avila, for some inexplicable reason I get the feeling that somehow you and I actually are alike. I'm quite prepared to dislike you if I must. I hope it doesn't become necessary.' He smiled, opened the door with unmistakable purpose and waited for the big man to depart.

Avila went to the door then turned. 'Just go, Doctor. Do whatever you must while you are here, then get your records completed and leave. And don't send back a hospital team, because if you do the hospital will burn to the ground some night, the people who run it will be without patients, and who knows—there may even be accidents happen.'

Leonard watched Avila stride across the entrance room and corridor. He followed at a discreet distance, saw Alfredo out there holding Avila's big horse. As the bearded big man took the reins he aimed a fierce blow with his quirt at Alfredo's legs and swung. Alfredo howled and sprang into the air. Alfredo mounted, looked at the cowboy, called him some rather stiff names in Spanish then shook the big quirt men-acingly and said in hissing Spanish: 'Go near that nurse once again, *vaquero*, and I swear to you I will dine on your liver!'

He wheeled and rode away.

Leonard turned back walking slowly and trying to make it all out. Somehow Nurse Cutler did fit in. How exactly, Leonard could only speculate. On the other hand these were healthy male animals and Nurse Cutler was exceptionally handsome.

'Doctor. . .?'

He saw her standing by the reception table. 'Coming, Nurse, coming.'

The actual removal of cataracts was not, normally, a difficult operation, nor did it entail the use of much time nor energy. But these were hardly normal work-ing conditions, for while Eloise had supervised the establishment of an operating facility by simply taking the smallest examination room out of use and converting it—having it scrubbed until it fairly reeked of disinfectant—there were certain definite drawbacks. One was the matter of good lighting. The moment he saw that naked bulb dangling from the ceiling he knew he'd have to improvise some changes of his own, which he did. Also, the table Nurse Cutler had found and brought to the room was not long enough, so a smaller table had to be brought in also, and scrubbed.

When he was satisfied an hour had gone by. Before he had inventoried everything that would be needed for both operative and post-operative care, another half hour was gone. Finally, when he had got himself ready, with Nurse Cutler to assist, more time had been used up. He could tell from Eloise Cutler's flattened lips she was annoyed by his thoroughness but he let that go by because obviously she'd never been a surgical nurse.

When all was in final readiness he stood across the table upon which the old man had been placed and looked her squarely in the eye. She looked straight back evidently expecting some comment about the operation. He said, 'Nurse, tell me something; how well do you know Avila?'

She was surprised by that question and showed it. 'Know him, Doctor. . .?'

He didn't reply. He just stood awaiting her answer.

She coloured and dropped her eyes to the unconscious patient, lifted them eventually and said, 'Only by sight—and reputation.'

He nodded. 'Then suppose we go to work.'

It was quiet in the little room. It was also rather warm but there was no help for that. He could have used one of the micrometer devices for measuring the growths to be removed. He could also have used a better facility, but he made out well enough without those things because he'd performed this same operation dozens of times.

When he finished he gave the instructions. 'Keep light away from his face. Make the bandage thick enough to preclude all light but soft enough to prevent pressure. Then put a nurse at his bedside for twenty-four hours.'

He left the little room, removed his surgical dress, washed vigorously and returned to his office to make a report. This latter matter, as he thought while doing it, was superfluous in a place like Puna, but a dedicated man went through all the motions out of strong habit.

Eventually, unaware that day was ending until he swung round to look out the window, he felt the need for a strong drink. He was not tired from the operation. He was feeling troubled, even frustrated, by the murky moods with which he was surrounded; by the atmosphere of suspicion, distrust, and in Avila's case, outright hostility.

When he arose to leave, a light hand knocked on the office door. He went across to open it. Eloise Cutler was standing there no longer attired in her crisp white cap and dress.

'I can report that the patient is doing well,' she said, eyeing him strangely, 'and I have put the private nurse on duty with him. But Doctor, we only have one full-time night nurse and two day nurses, so while we can do it this time, I'd like to suggest that in the future you make other arrangements for twenty-four hour help.'

He nodded dispassionately. 'I'm going round to the hotel for a drink. Could I prevail upon you to accompany me?'

She hesitated but only for a second or two. 'Thank you,' she said, 'I'll get my coat.'

He waited for her at the admissions desk—which was nothing more imposing than a rickety wooden table such as the one in his office. When she returned he led the way out into the cooling early evening. There wasn't a cloud in the sky but there was a steady, thin wind blowing off the snowfields far away that knifed through clothing. Two men were talking out front of the mayor's office but otherwise the plaza was deserted.

A gaunt old raffish dog jogged by, gave them a wide berth and kept an eye cocked towards them until he was out of stones'-throw. Several small chickens were industriously scratching in the dust. They also shied clear as Leonard and Eloise strolled past.

'Senility,' he said quietly, 'can very often be arrested by the removal of cataracts. Take away a person's sight, Miss Cutler, and it seems you very often take away their greatest single reason for living in the present.'

She wasn't thinking of the patient, evidently, for all she said was, 'He will recover. You must have performed that service dozens of times. You were very professional, Doctor.'

'And you, Nurse, have had little or no surgical experience.' She shot him a quick, hard look. He smiled blandly. 'It wasn't meant as a criticism, only as an observation. Never permit pride to interfere with learning, Miss Cutler.'

Mayor Sanchez came out of his office as they neared the hotel entrance, saw them, threw a brusque, unsmiling nod their way, locked his office door and went scurrying away.

'Now there,' Leonard said, halting to watch briefly, 'is a man with problems.'

'Avila,' she said. 'He is going to also be your problem, Doctor. You can bet on that.'

He considered the front of the old hotel. It had a surprisingly handsome and well-stocked bar. He's made that discovery the previous evening. He said, 'Do you live in this place too, Miss Cutler?'

'Yes. For outsiders it is here or nowhere.'

They entered, saw the few people inside the lobby glance quickly and with candid curiosity at them, passed on through to the bar and took a small table in a shadowy corner of the room.

The bar was very old. It had an atmosphere difficult to describe but the smell was the same odour once encountered in nearly every poorly ventilated bathroom anywhere on earth. Not unpleasant, especially, but definitely unhealthy. Still, no one can live forever, and there are times when the spirit needs bolstering at the expense of the liver. For Leonard Bordon this was such a time.

Chapter Six

Eloise wasn't particularly good company that evening. She asked him why he'd wanted to know how well she knew Avila. He told her:

'The man is either interested in you or doesn't want anyone else to be, which may amount to the same thing.'

He told her about Avila's quirt across the legs of the cowboy named Alfredo. She was definitely indignant but not angry. She had never, she told him, spoken to George Ritter Avila. As for Alfredo, he'd been only a patient and not a very good one at that.

She was quiet for a while after that. They both were. The liquor was rather good. Better than Leonard had expected to encounter in Magdalena Valley. A few people ambled in for a quick one then departed. The barman was an intelligent-looking light-complexioned mestizo with almost aristocratic features. When he brought over their second drinks he said, 'Doctor, it's good knowing you are here.'

Afterwards Leonard made a wry smile at Eloise. 'That's the first sincere welcome I've had.'

She was tart. 'And the moment someone whispers to him you are Jorge Avila's enemy he will look right through you.'

Leonard wasn't too perturbed. 'I wish I could sit down with Avila as you and I are sitting now.'

'It would be a waste of time, Doctor.'

He dropped the topic of Avila. As a matter of fact the man's name was beginning to bore him. 'Tell me about yourself, Miss Cutler.'

'I got carried away the same, I imagine, as you did, Doctor. I volunteered to help the under-privileged and here I am.'

He gently shook his head at her. 'Not quite that easily, Miss Cutler. With anyone as handsome as you there has to be more.'

She arched her dark brows at him.

He laughed at the warning in her eyes. 'No. I'm not trying to reach you through flattery. But I'd guess you to be perhaps twenty-five years of age and yet I notice you wear no rings. That doesn't make much sense. In any city I've been in you'd at least be engaged by now.'

She leaned back. 'I see. You must be a romanticist, Doctor, if you've pegged me as someone who is hiding a bruised heart. I've never been married nor engaged probably for the reason that I've never been in love.'

He still smiled. 'You haven't? It's very hard to believe, Nurse.'

'And you,' she shot back. 'Have you been in love, Doctor, or engaged—or married?'

'Not married nor engaged, Nurse, but I've been in love hundreds of times. As a child I wept for Ann Boleyn. I vowed vengeance against the slayers of my secret love, Mary, Queen of Scots. And when Gloria Swanson retired from the screen I went into seclusion for two days.'

She smiled. It was the first such expression she'd ever shown him. It made his spirit sing and his heart lighten its sombre beat. It also, incidentally, made her face light up with a beauty unmatched in his experience. She was without doubt the most completely beautiful woman he'd ever seen.

'You must have been an odd little boy, Doctor.'

He agreed. Right at the moment he'd have agreed with anything she'd said.

'And you *are* a romanticist.'

'Is that bad, Nurse?'

She lifted her glass, eyes narrowing slightly. 'I can't really say, Doctor. I've had very little experience in that field.'

He believed her but instead of saying so, which would have brought up the hardness to her eyes again, he asked if she wouldn't like some supper. She hung fire a moment before answering, studying him through those wide and narrowed eyes. He knew what she was doing: Probing for a clue that all this was some subtle approach of his leading up to something intimate later on. He could have dispelled the suspicion but didn't bother. He did, however, tell her that suspicious people missed an awful lot in life.

To reach the dining-room there was a sloping ramp. It was carpeted but Leonard got the impression that underneath was rammed earth instead of cement. Not that it mattered, really; it was just another of the bizarre blendings of this peculiar place—this entire large valley and all that was within it.

The food was good although for his taste somewhat overly seasoned. He didn't enquire—he'd learned long ago it was often better to enjoy food and not examine its antecedents too closely—but told Eloise it put him in mind of chicken cacciatore.

She looked up impishly. 'Goat, I'll wager my month's salary.'

'There is nothing more un-nerving than bluntness in a beautiful woman. I prefer thinking it's veal.'

She looked round at the sound of voices, looked back and wrinkled her nose. 'His Honour the Mayor,' she said, and returned to the meal.

He saw Sanchez, who was attired in a fresh suit and whose normal shadow was gone meaning that he'd shaved, and said, 'You don't like him.'

'Do you, Doctor?' she countered.

He told her approximately what he'd told Avila. 'I've only been here two days. I can't form opinions of people that fast.'

She narrowed her eyes again. 'You might try, Doctor. If you angered Jorge Avila today you may not have a lot of time left.'

He scoffed. 'The whip and machete don't particularly intimidate me, Miss Cutler. As for Mr Avila's size—it's impressive.'

'I didn't have physical violence in mind, Doctor,' she replied crisply. 'I had in mind a telephone call coming through directing you to return at once to Bogotá.'

He turned thoughtful. Avila had said something that dovetailed perfectly with her remark. The landowners bought the elected officials after elections. He asked if she had any personal knowledge that Avila had that much power.

She lowered her voice to answer. 'Mayor Sanchez, for one. He may not approve of the reactionarism, but he is owned body and soul by Avila which would mean he's been bought and paid for, Doctor. In Bogotá there will be others.'

He finished the meal and sat back. He wanted to

50

be able to say she was incorrect but he kept recalling those Land Reform posters. Leonard had seen the change come over Sanchez in a twinkling, when Avila rode up. He sighed.

'I'm afraid you may be right,' he told Eloise, arising to hold her chair and help her on with her coat. 'It's a bit discouraging, isn't it?'

'Wait,' she said, donning the garment then turning. 'Doctor, wait until you've been in a place like this as long as I have. Last year I came with a heart full of compassion. I didn't even see Jorge Avila the first four months. But I saw the people. They were apathetic, deceitful, apprehensive, distrustful—and dirty.'

He took her arm guiding her back towards the lobby and the velvet night beyond. He remembered Narcisso Pinzon's words about her. She continued speaking as soon as they were beyond ear-shot of the people inside the hotel.

'Filth and squalor and incredible indifference. I tried to explain. I even held classes in personal hygiene. Doctor, I now treat the ill, limit my advice, do what I must or what I can, and wait.'

'Wait. . .?'

'I agreed to stay one full year. It will be over next month.'

'And then?'

'Mister Avila can have Magdalena Valley for all I care. I simply want to go where there is cleanliness, understanding, efficiency again.'

He kept his arm hooked through her arm. He guided her in a slow stroll on around the west side of the darkened plaza. That little keening thin wind was gone but it still wasn't very warm. A gigantic moon began to rise from beyond the tallest mountain peaks. He paused to watch. It was the largest moon he'd ever seen.

'Immense,' he murmured.

The beauty was hauntingly exciting. Nothing and no man had changed a single line or furrow of those far-away gigantic mountains since the earth cooled millenias ago. He was looking at something out of the earliest times precisely as it had looked then.

She leaned a little so he could feel her closeness. He heard her breath softly run out. He knew the beauty was touching her deep down as it had him. Finally, when the moon was entirely up and away from the peaks, their ancient plateaux took on the weird and ghostly look of some other planet. They could look straight up the valley to those distant mountains and thrusting peaks without seeing a light, a fence, a house, a road of any kind, or even a lowly fire.

'As it was in the beginning,' he said. 'As it is now and as it shall always be.'

They passed along, had their view obstructed by a building and came slowly back to reality. But they had no more to say until, near the lower curve of the plaza, she paused to ask a question he could not properly answer.

'How is it that the only reasoning animal in Magdalena Valley is also the most miserable?'

'Why limit it to Magdalena Valley, Miss Cutler?'

They continued on round the plaza, slowed once where they caught the spicy smell of appetizing but not very nourishing food being cooked, and again, not far from the soldier-barracks where they heard a guitar making background music to a mournful song neither of them could understand.

They stopped out front of the hotel. 'Wait until you've been here a month or two,' she told Leonard. 'The enigma will reach you, Doctor.'

He understood what enigma she meant. It had reached him long before in a dozen different ways and he knew something about it she evidently had not yet discovered.

'It doesn't do a particle of good to become obsessed by its riddle, Miss Cutler. In the first place you're not going to find the answer. I doubt if anyone ever will. In the second place, ignorant, dirty and apathetic as these people are, they remain human beings. A thousand years of subjugation, slavery and total misery has made them this way. You and I won't change it very much but at least we can possibly help them take their first step up.'

She looked at him, slightly surprised to find he'd understood both her mood and her dilemma. 'Doctor, I feel so sorry for them—and so exasperated at the same time.'

'They know it, Miss Cutler.'

She looked away, up the long slot of the valley where the upthrusts still pointed to a soaring moon. She said nothing.

'I read a book about this part of the world on the flight out,' said Leonard. 'It began with the Spanish conquest. But I could close my eyes and see what it was like with people like these five hundred years before the Spaniards came—it was no different at all. In fact it was more cruel, more debasing. Well, you and I aren't going to become liberators in a couple of months or even in a year. But if we don't show them how to make the first hesitant step forward, we'll have failed dismally and damned if I came this far, gave up a good practice, just to fail. How about you?'

She shook her head while still avoiding his eyes. 'No, Doctor, I don't want to fail. Possibly I've tried to encompass the entire enormity of what must be done in my one tour of duty . . . I know they don't like me, Doctor.'

'Well, before either of us can do very much, Miss Cutler, we've got to take care of that. Agreed?'

Finally she looked at him. 'Agreed.'

He looked at his watch. It wasn't especially late but he was tired. 'Good night, Miss Cutler.'

'Goodnight, Doctor.'

They entered the hotel and parted in the lobby. On his way upstairs he smiled. He'd never fancied himself a proselyter but out there in front of the hotel he'd preached a pretty good sermon.

The hell of it was, as Narcisso Pinzon had bluntly said and as George Ritter Avila had definitely implied, if her public image couldn't be improved, what both she and Leonard Bordon were in Puna to accomplish was going to flatly fail.

He was drowsy and blamed it upon the two high-balls before supper. Tomorrow he'd begin compiling his report. With what records he'd already found at the dispensary it shouldn't take more than six or seven afternoons to do the entire thing. That of course would leave him quite a bit of spare time.

As he climbed into bed he thought that with any luck at all he could lend a considerable hand to Eloise Cutler in securing local goodwill. He closed his eyes, let go a big sigh and wondered what would happen if he tried to kiss Eloise.

Chapter Seven

The following day, his third in Magdalena Valley, he got no chance to begin compiling statistics for his report. The first thing in the morning a shrieking woman came to say her child had got badly burned. He and Eloise followed the woman back to her wretched hovel.

The child couldn't have been more than six or seven. She had pulled a boiling pot of cacao over upon herself. She'd have been a pretty child except for the horrible blisters which were forming as Leonard knelt beside her writhing form on the mud floor.

There were no clean rags in the house so he used a considerable amount of his precious bandaging material to cleanse and grease the child's face. Under his hands she ceased to whimper. By the time he was finished she could smile up at him from dark and trusting eyes.

When he got back to the dispensary the son of the old man for whom he'd removed the cataracts—himself past middle-age—came to ask after his father. Leonard went into minute detail explaining all that had been done. He took more time than he had, or than he should have taken, but when he sent the middle-aged man away with instructions not to return for another week, he had definitely made a friend. He had just as definitely impressed the mestizo with the

55

awesome ability of modern medicine.

Shortly after noon Eloise came to say Father Lopez wished to see him. He had the priest brought to his office. Eloise also told him she had two minor corrective surgeries for him to perform and would prepare their improvised operating room.

Father Lopez came with a springy stride, a boyish grin and an outstretched hand. 'I have a problem the church cannot handle, he said, accepting the chair Leonard offered.

'It must be quite a problem,' said Leonard, dropping down behind his table.

'It is. But first, tell me how it is working out, Doctor?'

'Fairly well, Father.'

'You are cautious.'

'Well, it pays under these circumstances.'

Father Lopez lost his smile. 'I was gambling that you were not too cautious a man, Dr Bordon.'

A faint warning tinkled in Leonard's head. 'Were you?' he asked politely. He leaned upon the rickety table. 'Could we get down to whatever brought you here, Father?'

'Yes, of course. I'm sorry. I know how busy you are. The burnt child this morning, two operations this afternoon, all the routine things between.'

Leonard sat waiting and studying the youthful priest. He didn't like the way Father Lopez's eyes jumped around seldom meeting his own stare. It gave him an instinctive bad feeling about their meeting.

'Well, Doctor, the ways of God are mysterious. I can usually guess what men are up to but seldom can I do as much with God.'

Leonard said nothing.

'Doctor, the church considers the taking of life a cardinal sin. Even unborn life. No man has the right to interfere in the workings of God. Even to save a mother's life. If she must die, then obviously this is the decree of God. She must die.'

Leonard very slowly straightened back off the table. He thought he knew what was coming.

'Doctor, the girl is not wed. She is frail and terribly frightened. She will kill herself, and of course that would also kill the child.'

'You want me to take the unborn child?' asked Leonard.

Father Lopez dropped his clipped head and said, 'Yes.'

Leonard knew some of what it had taken to make Father Lopez say that one word. He sat in quiet thought for a while. He was not, either in the religious or professional sense, committed to any such narrow precept as troubled Eusebio Lopez. He would take the child providing it were no more than embryo and providing the mother's own life would be unquestionably endangered if he did not. But this was a foreign nation. He did not know what national ethic might be violated. The people were, he'd been told, predominantly Catholic.

He would have to move very carefully here.

He told Father Lopez to bring the girl to him the following day, went with the priest to the roadway and left him there.

He did not mention Lopez's purpose for calling. At least not right then. He was too occupied for the next three hours anyway, for although neither minor surgery was critical in any sense, both consumed a lot of his time and all his concentration.

Afterwards, with an hour to himself, he began work

on the diary he was supposed to maintain—called a journal—while he was at Puna. He would have liked to go from there to the statistical report but one of the little dark day-nurses came to say Eloise wished to see him in her ward. He went dutifully, expecting trouble and was not disappointed in that respect.

'It is Alfredo again,' said Eloise, pointing to the dirty, rumpled, limp form outstretched upon an empty cot. 'He is drunk. Two men brought him in. They said he slipped and fell.'

Leonard went over to have a look. Alfredo reeked of liquor, his breathing was a bit queer and there was an odd little tic around one corner of his thick lips.

Eloise bent down to softly say, 'Brain damage?'

He didn't know, never made snap judgements, and straightened up to instruct her to have him cleaned up. Then he returned to the front of the dispensary to think. While he was standing near the door gazing out, over across the way he saw a lanky, light-complected soldier out front of the jailhouse talking to to a big man on a horse. Avila's back was to Leonard but he recognized the landowner nonetheless. On an inspiration he pushed out into the sunlight and walked over there. The soldier saw him first and growled something in a low voice. George Ritter Avila turned.

'Well Doctor,' he said, not unpleasantly, 'you are still here.'

Leonard let that pass. 'Mr Avila, I have your man Alfredo. He is being prepared for hospitalization. Were you aware...?'

Avila nodded. 'Yes. The fool thinks he is a mighty fighter after one drink. Half the men around have knocked him out one time or another.'

'Were you also aware he hadn't recovered from his last injury and this new one may be very serious for him?'

Avila relaxed in the saddle. 'Ahh. Doctor, you are telling me he could die.'

'Yes. If his brain has been injured again it is a very distinct possibility.'

'And what is it you want me to do?'

'Go to the mayor and tell him to release that young girl with the baby who is now in the jailhouse.'

Avila's dark brows climbed. The lanky soldier who'd been sullenly following the conversation, also showed astonishment. None of them had been discussing the girl; she hadn't been in at least two of the minds there.

Avila looked puzzled. 'Why, Doctor, what does the girl have to do with Alfredo?'

'Nothing. But she shouldn't be in that filthy place with her child. I rather doubted Mayor Sanchez would release her simply because I might wish it done.'

'But if I ask . . . ?'

'Exactly.'

Avila's bearded lips parted in a slow, hard smile. His tawny eyes also showed amusement. 'You have a devious mind,' he told Leonard. 'I may have underestimated you. All right. You shall have the girl and her child. For that small favour you will care for Alfredo.'

'Yes.'

Avila's lips lifted further disclosing white, strong teeth. 'Doctor, you would have cared for Alfredo anyway—no?'

Leonard grinned back. 'Yes. Now I've got to get back. Have the girl sent directly to the dispensary.'

As he walked away he could feel the gold-flecked eyes following him. Eloise was waiting just inside the front door. She didn't say anything right then, but led him over to the converted examination room where she had Alfredo laid out. Then she said, 'I don't think it's additional head damage at all, Doctor. He's so drunk he's limp as an old rag. There are only two bruises, one on the chest, one on the stomach.'

He went to work making the standard tests. There were a number he couldn't give because a drunk man's reflexes wouldn't properly respond, but as he finished with the examination he was convinced Eloise was correct. Alfredo had been struck twice, hard, and perhaps what had prevented additional head damage was the very limpness of his drunken condition. But in any case, he was not seriously hurt this time.

'Take him back,' Leonard said, moving away from their improvised operating table, 'and when he comes round let me know.'

She looked squarely at him. 'So you can tell George Ritter Avila, Doctor?'

'No, nurse, so I can tell Alfredo what I think of him.' He went to the door, turned back and said, 'And we'll have another boarder shortly. That child from the jailhouse with the emaciated baby I spoke to you about day before yesterday.'

'Yes,' she said, 'and what shall I do with her?'

'Use your own judgement, Nurse. I think in this case it might be superior to mine.'

He returned to the office. There were great huge shadows dropping out of the sky on all sides. Through his window he could see a thick woman gesturing to reluctant urchins at play in a mound of dirt. It was suppertime. He stood watching until the children and

60

the woman had disappeared into an adobe house, then turned back and saw the chair Father Lopez had used. It had not been moved since he'd been in it.

There were of course ways of inducing a miscarriage. In fact he could cause the girl to lose her child in such a fashion that it would appear a normal loss —except that she would lose it in his dispensary and even the Indians of Magdalena Valley were not that dense.

Something he'd noticed as a youth in school studying history. People could be outrageously abused, exploited, humiliated, even stared, and they would groan in submission. But let someone violate their religion and they turned into raging beasts.

If he took this child as Eusebio Lopez wished him to do, and the people discovered what he'd done and did not approve, only Leonard Bordon would be to blame in their eyes.

If it were just isolated Magdalena Valley the threat to his medical standing would be very remote, but this was the age of mass communication; if he stirred up a tempest in Puna it would become news all over the world.

Of course he hadn't committed himself to Father Lopez. For the matter of that he hadn't privately agreed he'd do any more than consider the case. He found himself wandering what Eloise Cutler's reaction would be —and thought he knew; thought he could imagine the chilling stare she'd turn on him.

He uttered a short, harsh laugh because, out of memory, came the bland, smooth face of Dr Francisco Ariano, London-educated Director of Health and Welfare, back in Bogotá.

'*It will be dull down there as a matter of fact, Dr*

Bordon. Dull and routine. The people are docile, friendly. You will be bored to tears before your two months are up.'

He reached for his coat, adjusted his necktie in a small wall-mirror and called Dr Ariano and a good old-fashioned, unprintable Saxon name.

Outside, the evening was bland and warm. It was the first truly warm night he'd experienced since arriving in Magdalena Valley. He thrust both hands into trouser pockets and went plodding up towards the hotel for a drink, supper, and bed. At least those three things were routine. It was the things which happened between which were troublesome.

That same light-complected barman was on duty. He fixed Leonard's highball on sight, placed it upon the countertop and smilingly said, 'There is only one of you, Doctor; there is a whole town of us. That is how we know who you are. That is how I remember what you drink.'

Leonard smiled, thanked the barman and paid him. He then sat there sipping rum and lemon wondering whether Eloise Cutler had expected him to ask her to supper again tonight.

He would have; in fact he'd have been pleased to have asked her, but also he doubted that she would have come. She was a discreet woman as well as beautiful. She would say, 'It will become a habit, Doctor.' Or, 'We will start people talking.' Perhaps she'd simply say, 'I'd prefer not to become too involved, Doctor.'

He liked that last sentence the best because it was cool, forthright, and—

'Good evening, Doctor.'

He turned. She was nodding at the barman who

began at once to mix her favourite highball. She took the stool next to Leonard.

'I missed you at quitting time, Doctor.'

He was thrown into confusion by her warmth and easy amiability. All he could think to do was sit there inanely smiling at her, wordless.

Chapter Eight

George Ritter Avila brought the big-eyed, filthy little mother clutching her listless child to the dispensary himself. He was without either quirt or machete but the girl, cringing from his size and bearded, villainous appearance, was in terror of him nonetheless.

Avila pushed the girl into Leonard's office, growled a command which sent her at once to a chair, then stood towering, and shrugged at Leonard. In English, which obviously the girl didn't understand, Avila said, 'She has vermin, Doctor. I'd disinfect her first. Her name is Felicidad—some name for a girl of her trade, eh? Anglicize it if you wish; call her Felicity or Phyllis. How is Alfredo?'

'Would you care to see him? He's going to be fine.'

'No, I don't want to see the dog. I might bust his head anew. Whenever I need him he's down here in Puna making a fool of himself.'

'I'm obliged for what you've done, Mr Avila,' said Leonard rising to move from behind the table.

The big man dropped a glance upon the ragged, thin and listless girl. 'Don't thank me, Doctor. I am not your friend. I want you out of here.'

'Even though I'm no threat to you?'

'You *are* a threat. Any hospital would be a threat.'

'That's ridiculous, Mr Avila. Hospitals aren't political.'

'You're wrong, Doctor. To teach these people hygiene you'll have to first teach them to read. As soon as they can do that, they will get books.'

Leonard looked into the big man's tawny eyes and said, 'Mr Avila, I don't believe you can possibly be as tyrannical as that statement makes you sound. Moreover, since you are no fool, you know damned well you can't stop the hospital from coming any more than you can stop the Land Reform Program—or the schools which will follow. If I were you I'd be a leader in the new era—not an enemy of it.

Avila's wide mouth lifted mirthlessly. 'Doctor, you have no investment here. You can talk like a liberal; you can't lose either way.'

'Can you, Mr Avila? The government will reimburse you for the land. There is a state bonus and—'

'We've been over this before, Doctor. Goodbye.'

Avila stamped out leaving Leonard with the girl. He knew it was pointless but he asked her name in English nonetheless. She sat and watched him from lacklustre big black eyes. He poked his head out into the corridor and called for someone.

One of Eloise's little pudgy, dark nurses came, blinked in surprise at sight of the girl, and looked inquiringly at Dr Bordon. He asked if she knew the girl. She replied in English that she knew her, of course; everyone in Puna knew her. She was a *puta*. No one knew who her parents were. Something very matter-of-fact in the nurse's attitude irritated Leonard. He told the nurse to take the girl out and see that she was thoroughly bathed, her hair shaved, and that she was disinfected. Then she was to see that the baby was similarly treated, after which she was to reunite them and see that they were both fed with the dispensary employees.

The nurse agreed without saying so—with little bobs of her head—with all but those last orders. She looked at Leonard a trifle sullenly. He did not relent. After escorting the nurse and girl out of his office he went in search of Eloise.

She was having tea in a corner of her ward which had been curtained off to form a canvas-walled private cubicle. He told her of the girl and his orders respecting her. She said nothing but offered him tea, which he declined. She sat at a tiny table, looked at some forms she'd been filling out when he'd entered, and finally she looked at him.

'If you begin, Doctor, there just is no end to it, and we simply do not have the help, the facilities, nor the budget.'

'That's why I'm here,' he told her. 'To determine those things.'

'All anyone needs, Doctor, is two reasonably good eyes to see with, and an unbiased mind to make decisions with. That's all. I've been making a marginal notes on my monthly reports for almost a year and nothing has happened.'

'I'm here, Miss Cutler. Those notes must have impressed someone.'

'Well, to get back to Phyllis—or whatever her name is—I anticipated this since you first mentioned the child. We are ready for her.'

He smiled. 'I thought you might be, Miss Cutler.'

Their eyes met and held until she suddenly looked away. He softly said, 'That first step upwards, remember?' and walked back out into the ward.

He didn't see her again until mid-afternoon when she came to say Phyllis had been cared for, examined and fed, and that her baby, while very emaciated, was a hardy little thing.

'T.L.C.' She murmured in the doorway of his office. 'Tender loving care. I think that is fundamentally what they both need. I know that look she has in her eye. Complete defeat; total surrender to an overwhelming, bleak fate. It still makes me want to cry when I see it.'

He left his work at the table and crossed the room. 'We won't cry about it, Miss Cutler, damned if we will. We'll do something about it.' He thought a moment then said, 'I want you to go to supper with me again tonight. I have something to tell you.'

She nodded and left. Fifteen minutes later when he was engrossed in compiling the initial draft of his report, Mayor Elfego Sanchez came to call upon him. He very resignedly put aside the papers again, offered Sanchez a chair and waited. Clearly, the mayor was upset about something. When it finally came out, Leonard sat petrified in his chair.

'. . . All I know, Doctor, is that when my daughter ran away she left a note saying she would take her life if I sent the soldiers hunting her. Now I can't imagine what this is all about, but here is the note. Pardon me, Doctor; do you read Spanish?'

Leonard shook his head but he didn't have to be able to read the note to know what it said. Father Lopez had already told him. When he recovered from the shock he asked two questions of Sanchez.

'Does your daughter have a fiancé, Mr Sanchez, and does she fancy herself in love?'

The mayor nodded, but being innocent of what Leonard had in mind, he simply said, 'Yes, but then there's been no fight. I saw the boy last night. He had no idea where our Elena has gone. I think she must be sick, Doctor, which is why I've come to you. She must be delirious, perhaps.'

Leonard waited, letting Elfego Sanchez talk on. It took a little while for his shock to pass. Also, he was annoyed at Father Lopez. It was one thing to abort some dull-witted Indian girl whose parents might not even be alive, but who in any case could only feel gratitude. It would be something altogether different to abort Mayor Sanchez's daughter, whom Father Lopez was obviously hiding in the cathedral.

After a while he got rid of Sanchez saying that if and when the girl were found, she should be brought to him for an examination. Sanchez, still dazed, agreed and left.

Leonard returned to his statisitical report but it was hard to keep his mind on the pages. Eventually, at noon, he left the dispensary without telling anyone where he was going, and paid a call upon Father Lopez at the cathedral. The day was warm but the great old mud church was as impartially cool as always—and just as silently empty and brooding.

He laid it on the line to Father Lopez; told him who the girl was Lopez was shielding, and also told him that the girl should go to her parents with her troubles, not involve men who se entire careers could be ruined for helping her.

Father Lopez didn't argue. He simply took Leonard out back to the great, long patio across the rear of his church, sat him on the same ancient oaken bench, and said, 'Doctor; Elfego Sanchez will kill the boy. His daughter is so distraught already there isn't a doubt in my mind she will kill herself. Then of course there is the army: Elfego Sanchez does not belong to the proper clique. The army will arrest him for murder. Now Doctor, it is these things I've considered. I realize the risk to myself. I am prepared to take it. Before I'd have involved you further I'd have have explained the entire situation to you. But is it better in the eyes of man and God to see four people die, or just one? That is what I've prayed about since yesterday morning when I found Elena Sanchez in front of the High Altar hysterically beseeching forgiveness for what she was about to do—with an old knife in her hand. The shock that she'd have done it right there, defiling the church, horrified me only a little more than that she meant to do it.'

Leonard listened attentively. He could sympathize with Father Lopez, but still, the risk was overwhelming. And of course there was the ethical consideration: He could take the embryo without a qualm, but not under any guise of deceit. He said, 'Father; Sanchez will have to know. You can't be a party to anything as dishonest as this and neither can I. I sympathize with the girl, but I will not be involved in anything as dishonest as this at all.'

Leonard would have arisen but Father Lopez restrained him with a hand upon his sleeve. 'Think of the boy, Doctor. Sanchez will kill him. He will *have* to do that.'

Leonard was briefly pensive, then said, 'Does the girl really love this boy?'

Father Lopez grimaced. 'She despises him. She goes into paroxysms of tearful remorse at the mention of his name.'

'What is his name, Father?'

Lopez's black eyes widened on Leonard. 'No,' he softly said. 'No, Doctor; you can't do that; you can't tell Sanchez his name.'

'I didn't have any such thing in mind. I simply want

69

to know who the embryo's father is.'

'To turn over to the soldiers?'

'No. Not to turn over to anyone. Just to know.'

'Well. It is Roberto Gomez.'

Leonard left Father Lopez, walked back to the dispensary and nearly collided with Jorge Avila emerging. The big man's tawny eyes were ironic. When Leonard asked if Avila had been seeking him, Avila shook his head.

'Alfredo, the pig. I was in town so stopped to see if he had died yet. Worse luck, I am told he will be all right.'

'I need another favour of you,' said Leonard.

'If you will promise to go away, Doctor,' said Avila, grinning.

'I'll go when two months have passed. I've already told you that. I need someone to find a youth named Roberto Gomez and bring him to my office in the dispensary.'

Avila stood thoughtfully eyeing Leonard. Bordon was nearly as tall but he lacked a foot of being as wide as Avila. Finally the landowner said, 'All right. But now you will owe me something, Dr Bordon. Is that agreed?'

Leonard squirmed. 'Within reason, yes.'

Avila looked up and down the late-day roadway. He sighed. 'Do you know what I think, Doctor; I think you are going to bring a hospital anyway.' The gold-flecked eyes swung back. 'I got news today. A land reform team with soldiers is on its way here. It seems the reform program in Magdalena Valley is going too slowly.' Avila looked down the road again and said, 'Well, now it comes, Doctor. Keep your beds prepared and your medicines handy. Now it comes.'

Avila strode away without actually ever saying whether he'd bring in Roberto Gomez or not, and Leonard forgot Gomez anyway, as he stood watching the big man depart.

Inside, he met Eloise and asked her to come into his office. He'd meant to leisurely tell her about the pregnant girl later, after work-hours and when they could relax at the hotel. Now, he felt an impelling urgency about the affair.

He closed the door carefully behind her, held a chair, then started telling what he knew and watching her face. She showed astonishment only once, that was when he told the girl's name—Elena Sanchez—but otherwise she sat and listened, as composed as any professional nurse would be.

When he'd finished she crossed her legs, smoothed her skirt and said, 'Doctor, are you asking for my personal feelings, or do you want some idea of local reaction to an abortion?'

He'd thought he'd guessed her personal reaction earlier. Nevertheless he said, 'Both.'

'Personally, I favour the abortion.'

He was surprised.

'Otherwise, I frankly don't think the Indians and mestizos would care one way or another. They just don't have that much religion any more. But I may be wrong, and if I am, Doctor, do you realize what you're putting on the chopping block? Your reputation, your livelihood, your lifelong profession!'

Chapter Nine

Oddly enough when Roberto Gomez arrived to see Dr Bordon he was in the company of that same chunky, cold-eyed soldier who'd been on guard outside the jail-house the day Leonard had arrived in Puna. The soldier had his little ugly sub-machine gun slung from a shoulder. He didn't smile, in fact he acted sullen, but he prodded the youth into Leonard's office anyway, obviously doing his duty but for some reason person-ally averse.

The soldier left and Leonard sat gazing at the cause of Elena Sanchez's predicament. He was an Indian, tall and lean and narrow-chested. His eyes were opaque black, his features, although good, were loose and flaccid. His hairline almost met both black eye-brows. Leonard read that face precisely, sighed and motioned Gomez to a chair.

The gangling youth sat but his facial expression didn't change. He had the look of a trapped animal. Leonard wondered about the language barrier.

'Your name is Roberto Gomez,' he said.

The youth nodded, which proved at least that he understood English. Leonard sat silent for a moment grouping his words. He knew exactly what he would say because he'd been thinking about it since his visit with Father Lopez.

'Roberto, you are aware Elena Sanchez had run away.'

Another non-committal nod and no flicker at all in the obsidian eyes. The boy was still fearful, but now he was being cagey as well.

'And you know *why* she ran away.'

This time the youth sat like stone, evidently unwilling to implicate himself by even so much as a nod.

Leonard wasn't concerned. He hadn't exactly expected Gomez to lie anyway. He said, 'Well, I know where she is.'

That time the black eyes flickered—but with fear, not relief.

'You don't care about her, do you?'

The black eyes turned opaque again. Gomez wasn't going to speak until he knew what direction this conversation was likely to take.

'She doesn't care about you—now. So I'm going to give you a way out. Otherwise you know what her father will do if he finds out.'

'I know,' said the Indian, speaking for the first time.

'And you don't care about her, do you?'

'No, *Señor*.'

'All right, Roberto.' Leonard fished in a pocket, brought forth a slim, crisp packet of paper money. 'Get out of Puna, Roberto,' he said, sliding the money across the table. 'Leave Magdalena Valley. Never return. Do you understand? *Never* return. Because by this time tomorrow Elfego Sanchez will know about you and his Elena.'

The black eyes clung to the money but Gomez made no move to take it. He licked his lips, looked Leonard squarely in the eyes and said, 'I would have gone a

73

week ago, when she told me, *Señor*. I would have gone yesterday when I knew something was going to happen. But I had no money.'

'You have it now. Take it.'

Gomez picked up the bills, felt them carefully and considered the amount. It was more than enough to get him out of the country; he could even live for a month or two on what was left after paying his way to the border. He licked his lips again. His whole attitude changed. He looked enormously relieved.

'I will leave in Narcisso Pinzon's car tonight,' he said.

Leonard looked surprised. 'Pinzon is coming back tonight?'

'*Si*. He telephoned that he would be here tonight with your supplies. Then he will go back. I will go with him.'

Leonard leaned back and gazed at the young Indian. He wanted to know more about the boy but he didn't ask because he was uncomfortable over what he'd just done. It wasn't simply a matter of saving Roberto Gomez from Elfego Sanchez's pistol or knife or shotgun; it was also a very serious matter of helping Gomez escape, which, should Sanchez ever learn about it, might put Dr Bordon in Gomez's place.

But what else could he do? Nothing, he told himself, nothing at all; if Sanchez found out and came for him—well—he'd have to try and talk himself out of the mess.

He arose, pointed to the door and said, 'Roberto, if you aren't gone by tomorrow morning I'll see that Sanchez knows it was you. Now go on; get out of here.'

The Indian arose, moved like a panther to the door, turned with a hand on the knob and soberly considered his benefactor. *"Gracias,"* he said, sounding doubtful. "I know how it is with people like you. It's not that way with us. But I owe you thanks anyway.'

After the door closed Leonard rummaged his pockets, found another packet of money, counted it ruefully and swore under his voice. It would be adequate but now he'd have no reserve. Of course in Bogotá they'd assured him he wouldn't need a reserve in Puna because there was no place to spend money; very much of it at any rate. But they'd also told him other things in Bogotá which had been proved false.

Eloise came by at five o'clock to look in on him. He was working on the reports. She said if he'd prefer, they could go to supper some other night. He sprang up, grabbed his coat and shrugged into it.

'I need your company tonight; just let me straighten my tie.'

Outside, the day was ending and up the far reaches of the valley those selfsame giant, jagged peaks were hiding the moon again. There was nothing up there as far as they could see. He was saturnine about that.

'What in the name of Holy Harry does Avila want to keep that kind of land for?'

She looked at him. 'Not *that* land, Doctor. That's uncultivated. The big landowners have their *estancios* north and west of Puna.'

As they started towards the hotel she said she'd have to see about renting a car to take him over the countryside. He wasn't enthusiastic.

'I've seen enough of Magdalena Valley.'

'But it's beautiful; it's a fairyland where the estates are.'

Something that had been bothering came to the fore in his thoughts. 'Tell me, why is it always only Avila

75

I see? Why don't the other landowners come around?'

'Jorge Avila is the only one who lives here year round. The others are absentee landlords. That's what started all this business about land reform. The absentee landlords live in Bogotá, or Buenos Aires. Some even winter in Florida and summer in Europe. I don't feel sorry for them. If they'd paid these people a living wage I doubt that this would have happened. Avila is the only one who pays decently. These people fight to work for him.'

He looked at her, his eyes perplexed. 'I can't figure him out. He bluffs everyone with that loaded whip and machete. Yet Alfredo worships him and now you say others do as well.'

'He can make this a battlefield or he can make it a peaceful settlement. It will all depend on what action he takes when the land reform people arrive.'

'They'll be here tomorrow. Avila told me that himself. And they are coming with soldiers.'

She dropped her eyes to the ground over which they walked and had no more to say until they were out front of the hotel. Then she stopped, looking up as though surprised where she was, and turned towards him.

'Can we walk a little or are you terribly hungry?'

He wasn't the least bit hungry and he told her why. 'I gave the boy who got Elena Sanchez into trouble one hundred U.S. dollars to get out of the country and stay out.'

She was stunned. *"A hundred dollars?* Doctor; that's more than he could make in six months.'

'That's not important. I had to get him out of here before Sanchez finds out what's wrong with his damned Elena and shoots the boy.'

She hooked her arm through his. He was surprised at the intimacy but he didn't resist at all. She said, 'Of course that puts you into it up to your chin. You realize that of course?'

'Of course. What would you have done?'

She didn't answer. 'And about the girl; will you perform the operation?'

He had no idea. 'I don't think so. I haven't seen her but I don't think I can allow myself to get involved. I'm here for just one purpose.'

She said slowly, 'Doctor, I've been through this before. Not here, but everything is about the same. I'm not saying I favour indiscriminate abortion, but I *will* say that for a child to be born whose parents and grandparents will despise what he stands for, and all the people for miles around will know what he is, isn't going to help that child grow into any kind of worthwhile individual.

'There was a child here years ago. I didn't know him of course but I've heard the story a dozen times. His name was Teofilo. In the massacre fifteen or twenty years ago he saw soldiers hack his parents to bits with machetes. He went into the mountains. By the time he was eighteen he'd killed three hundred people. He didn't even know them. Mostly, they were innocent farmers and herdsmen, of course many were also soldiers. They killed him one night and burned his body.'

Leonard said quietly, 'All right, Eloise, you've made your point. Now let's go have a highball.' He swung her round heading back towards the lighted hotel. A big man on a dark horse rode past. He saw them and raised a mighty arm from which dangled the shot-loaded quirt. They nodded back. Jorge Avila turned off down a little roadway and dropped from sight.

'Tomorrow,' she whispered, and gave a little shudder he could feel. 'I don't like Jorge Avila. I don't trust him nor like him at all.'

Leonard said nothing. He didn't agree with her assessment of Avila but he couldn't have said exactly *why* he didn't agree with it. Perhaps it was something only another man would have understood. He didn't even know the word *macho*, but if he'd ever heard it defined he'd have known at once it described big, powerful and wealthy Jorge Avila perfectly. *Macho* meant 'man', but in a very special way. *That* kind of man was *all* man; he would fight, he would kill, he was fearless but he was also intelligent and shrewdly understanding. There was no word to quite cover what *macho* meant in English.

They took their corner table and at once the light-complected mestizo barman brought their usual drinks. Leonard sipped, felt the warmth, and said, 'Listen, I want you to disassociate yourself from this mess. I don't want you to be involved in any way.'

She watched his eyes and said, 'You are something more than I thought, Doctor. I'm not even sure you and Jorge Avila aren't a little alike.'

He set the glass aside, leaned back and gazed at her. The lighting wasn't very good. In shadow like that she looked very young; as she must have looked at fifteen or sixteen.

'Don't dig,' he said. 'Just keep out of what is coming.'

'I don't think I'll do that,' she said very softly and slowly. She smiled at him. 'You're the first person I've met in almost a year who *knew* what should be done and was willing to do it.'

'I didn't say I'd do it.'

She still smiled. 'But you will, Doctor.'

He finished his drink, arose and said, 'Let's go eat.' He spoke savagely as though the meal would be something he'd made up his mind about and, unpleasant though it was bound to be, he would intentionally go through with it.

She approved. He didn't realize that at the moment but later on, lying awake in the darkness of his bedroom, he knew she had approved. That made him groan. It was one thing for a man to gamble everything for a foolish principle. It was quite another to drag someone else down with him. It hadn't been supper he'd been feeling savage towards and she'd known that too. Remarkable woman, Eloise Cutler.

Chapter Ten

One of Eloise's nurses came to report that Felicidad
was ill. Eloise and Leonard were discussing several
recent patients together, so they went the same way
to see the girl and found her crying into a pillow while
her wizened child blissfully slept in a basket on the
floor beside her bed.

They had to get one of the nurses to interpret. What
it all amounted to was that Felicidad knew they were
going to keep her head shaved from now on so that
when she was released from the hospital no men would
look at her. Then she and her child would starve for
there was no other work.

Eloise knelt, took the girl's hand and held it as she
spoke through her interpreter saying, 'You can stay
here as long as you like, and when your hair grows
back we'll buy you a fine dress. We only shaved your
head to kill all the lice. And look at your son; he sleeps
formidably for the first time in months, I'll wager.'

Tears stopped but the frightened, pinched face was
still distrustful. Leonard drew Eloise away. 'You can
only do so much at one time. It was enough right then
making her stop weeping. Next time—something else.
She is a bright child.'

'An *experienced* child, Doctor,' said Eloise tartly as
she left him at the door to her ward. 'It's enough to
shrivel the heart of a person.'

He caught a wisp of a baggy white suit whipping round the corner in the direction of the roadway door and said, with a sigh, 'I'll check back with you a bit later,' and walked towards his office to intercept Elfego Sanchez.

The mayor was in worse shape than he'd been in the night before. If he'd got any sleep at all the previous night it clearly hadn't been enough; there were grey bags under each eye, his expression was etched with mournful anxiety, his step was faltering, like the step of a half-drunk.

Leonard took him into the office and got him a chair. He felt like spanking a girl he'd never seen—and a priest too. He got some watered whiskey for Sanchez, then went round to take his seat behind the table. They'd exchanged meaningless greetings. Sanchez said next: 'Doctor, she didn't come back. I don't know what to do. Her mother is becoming very ill. You must understand, Elena is our only child. We are not young people any more; there will never be another.' Sanchez sipped his watered whiskey. It was strong enough to float a horseshoe and after a bit it became difficult for Leonard to tell which were his real tears and which where liquor-inspired tears.

'. . . We went to see the priest, Doctor. . .'

'What did he tell you?'

Sanchez finished the watered whiskey, set the glass aside and made a floppy gesture with one upraised arm. 'You know what priests tell people, Doctor. I've heard those same things said ever since I was a small child. We are to "believe" to have "faith", to understand that our Elena's disappearance is the mysterious working of High Fate. Well, Doctor, we don't care for any of that talk, we only want her back. We would give anything. . .'

Leonard waited until the voice began to be a point-less monotone then he took Mayor Sanchez and got rid of him. He was returning across the entrance room towards his office when a familiar voice called softly. He turned and saw Narcisso Pinzon grinning from the doorway.

Leonard was electrified. He'd been under the impression Pinzon wasn't to arrive until evening; at the very earliest in the afternoon. It was now barely mid-day.

Pinzon walked on up. 'I have some soldiers unload-ing your crates, Doctor, so I thought I should come round and pay my proper respects.'

'I was told you wouldn't get here until evening, Narcisso.'

Pinzon shrugged. 'The wind was at our back, Doctor. Moreover there were several trucks of the army. We made excellent time.'

Leonard jerked his head. 'Come into my office,' he said, leading the way.

The Indian was at ease, and yet he was also deferen-tial. He'd always treated Leonard with marked respect. It had nothing at all to do with race, but rather pro-fession. Medical practitioners were known as vastly learned men. Among people such as Columbians who equate education with intelligence those who study longest are accorded most respect. When Leonard asked Narcisso to be seated he remained standing, holding his old hat and looking fondly at his host.

Without any preliminary he said, 'Well, Doctor; you didn't meant to, of course—I wasn't sure about that —but you have become a fixture in Magdalena Valley.'

'Hardly a fixture,' murmured Leonard, dropping

into his chair and believing Narcisso had used the word 'fixture' because he couldn't find the appropriate English word. He was wrong.

'Yes, Doctor, a fixture. The first thing I heard this morning when I climbed from the car was that you'd performed a miracle—you'd restored the eyesight to the old one, Raymondo Reyes.'

'A simple operation, Narcisso.'

"For you, perhaps. To these people—a miracle." Narcisso raised a hand. 'Not magic. They are not completely ignorant, but medicine that can restore eyesight is miraculous. You must have at one time thought so yourself.'

Leonard switched the topic. 'What supplies did you being?'

'All that you left behind as well as additional boxes I was given at the INCORA office. And this.' Narcisso fished out a bulky, limp envelope and handed it across. 'I was instructed by no one less than the Director himself to hand you that letter, *Señor*."

Leonard smiled. 'I am grateful, *amigo*.'

'Doctor; a question if I may: You have the girl Felicidad Osmena here?'

Leonard didn't know Felicidad's last name, had never heard it that he knew of. He nodded. 'We have the girl named Felicidad from the jailhouse here. And her child.'

Narcisso nodded without additional coment. 'And *Señor* Avila—you two have met?'

'Several times,' Leonard replied dryly. 'I have his man Alfredo here.'

Narcisso nodded. 'Yes, I know.'

Leonard shook his head. Narcisso had heard quite a bit since his very recent arrival. He said, 'Alfredo

83

can be released in another day or two. Avila can have him back.'

'I am grateful, Doctor. Alfredo is my brother.'

That *did* stun Leonard. He almost said something, too, but he controlled himself. Narcisso was a shrewd and observant man. He slowly smiled. 'I know, Doctor. I know. Well, it's not possible for a man to pick his relatives, is it?'

'What of the soldiers you brought?' asked Leonard, getting clear of the subject of Alfredo Pinzon.

'Thirty-five, Doctor. They are to go with the land surveyors and officials of the reform to make certain landowners don't ambush them. With the soldiers already here, it makes quite a fighting force. Fifty men, Doctor.'

Leonard told him Avila knew the troops were coming. He also recounted what Avila had said the night before. Narcisso glumly nodded. He already knew what warlike talk had been going around. He also said something that echoed the opinion of someone else.

'The fools will fight against these soldiers if Jorge Avila tells them to. And yet these land reform people are here to give those fools free land. Twelve and one-half acres to each family. Jorge Avila is a very powerful man. That's what I told the *teniente* on the ride here. In a fight he could perhaps get a hundred men.'

'And what did the lieutenant say?'

'What do young lieutenant always say, Doctor? I have come to serve my *patria*; to do my duty; if need be to die gloriously in the service of my fatherland. Doctor, has it ever seemed to you people die very easily and very foolishly?'

Leonard couldn't keep from laughing at the plaintive tone and the long face of Narcisso Pinzon. 'It has often occurred to me,' he agreed. 'Narcisso, go see that the supplies are properly tucked away, then come back to my office this evening. I have something to tell you that you won't like. Meanwhile, I'm going to see if I can't keep a war from starting here.'

'You? How, Doctor?'

'I don't know.'

Now it was Pinzon's turn to smile. 'That is very sound strategy,' he murmured, and retreated through the doorway still grinning.

Eloise, seeing Narcisso, knocked and entered. He told her of the fresh supplies, asked her to have a chair and opened the thick envelope. There were several cheques—one for Eloise which he handed over. There were some fresh directives which were as applicable as any directive would have been under the circumstances. And finally there were two personal letters, one begging him to co-operate to the fullest with the land reform team, the other letter blandly informing him that the request for a hospital in Magdalena Valley had been approved and would he kindly forward, at once, the statistics he'd no doubt compiled by this time which would support the need. *That* letter he smoothed out on the old table in front of himself and uttered one harmless swear word about.

'Why in the hell,' he exclaimed, 'send anyone here at all if they already knew they would establish a hospital at Puna?'

Eloise, who didn't know what was in the letter, arose and smiled. 'Because perhaps the clairvoyant seers in Bogotá actually did read all my little marginal pleas, Doctor.'

He doubted that very much; from long experience

with bureaucracy he knew how the civil service mind worked; it was *not* original in any sense.

Then she said, 'I'd better go see where they are putting the fresh supplies,' hesitated a moment, looked at him and concluded with: 'The town is full of armed soldiers, Doctor.'

He swept the offending letter away and arose. 'I know.'

'Well, don't you think it might be dangerous to make any revelations right now?'

'Revelations, Miss Cutler?'

'The Sanchez matter.'

He thought he knew what she meant. She doubted the wisdom of bringing Elena Sanchez to the dispensary at this time, or of letting the mayor know anything at all. 'You may be right, Eloise. They are an unpredictable people. By the way—dinner tonight?'

She smiled and went to the door. 'We will become alcoholics,' she said. 'I'll come by and remind you at five o'clock.'

He nodded absently and followed her on out. She went briskly towards her ward, he went towards the admissions desk and was caught there by a handsome, youthful, crew-cut mestizo in lace boots and khaki clothing who cheerily introduced himself as 'Dr Eduardo Lleras, local director of the Land Reform Program under the Columbian Institute of Agragrian Reform.'

Leonard couldn't repress the smile and Dr Lleras chuckled. It was a matter of liking one another on first sight. Lleras said, 'The title makes up for the poor pay. And I'm an educational doctor, not a medical doctor, so I think while I'm here I'd better be just plain Ed Lleras.'

The Columbian's English was flawless, but it was U.S.-English, not English-English. They talked for a while, discussing Lleras's task, and only once did the youthful, buoyant Lleras show concern. That was when he mentioned Jorge Ritter Avila. 'Dr Bordon the last thing I want in Magdalena Valley is a war. I'm going to drive out to see *Señor* Avila this afternoon. He's got to be enlightened.'

That last word made Leonard's eyes ironically darken. 'If I could, Dr Lleras, I'd like to ride along. And as for "enlightening" *Señor* Avila...' Leonard wagged his head. 'He is older than you, and he's highly intelligent. He is very complex and...I don't know exactly how to describe him, but don't go out there expecting to find some old time *bandolero* with armed men all round and horse-cavalry.'

'Would you object to calling me simply Ed, Doctor?'

'I'd be honoured, Ed.'

'As for Avila...' the youthful shoulders rose and fell. 'I'll get down on my knees if I must.'

'Don't threaten him, Ed.'

'All right. Any other advice?'

'No. That's why I'd like to ride along. To perhaps help in some way. But I'm not sure he isn't a match for both of us.'

Ed Lleras's broad, boyish smile returned. 'I'll be here for you within a couple of hours, Doctor.'

Leonard, watching Ed Lleras depart, began for the first time to feel as though this might not be an entire journey through darkness. If only Jorge Avila would warm to the very sincere, effervescent Director as Leonard had.

'The hell of it was with a man like Avila one never knew exactly where one stood. Leonard didn't know

87

even though Avila had repeatedly said he was not Leonard's friend—then he had turned right around and had done him favours. One thing Leonard was certain of: It all lay in the huge hand of Jorge Avila, whatever happened.

Chapter Eleven

Lieutenant Honorio Elizondo was also youthful, but he had little humour in him. He was a *creole,* a Latin American of pure Spanish descent born in South America. He was a trifle stiff even with Leonard who had to be his equal, so it was reasonable to assume with inferiors he'd be a strict disciplinarian. It was always puzzling to understand how professional soldiers of tiny countries with insignificant armies could be this way, for in a real fight almost anyone could whip them.

But perhaps that's what was required. At any rate Honorio Elizondo told Dr Bordon in no uncertain terms he had the men and, more important, the weaponry, to compel obedience to the Central Government, and he meant to see the George Ritter Avila, as leader of the rebellious element, obeyed the law.

Leonard, uneasy in the face of this kind of attitude, tried soothing words. 'Lieutenant Elizondo, I'm going out to see *Señor* Avila this afternoon. I suggest you keep your armed men in the city until I've had my chance. The last thing we both want to see is bloodshed.'

Elizondo wasn't entirely compatible. 'I'll let the soldiers rest, Doctor, but as for the bloodshed—that's my job.'

Later, after the officer had left, Leonard stood by his

office window thinking Honorio Elizondo was precisely the type soldier that *wasn't* needed in Magdalena Valley.

Eloise came to see him shortly after noon. Alfredo, she said, had been visited by Narcisso Pinzon, and now Alfredo was very contrite; he'd apologized to her —for what, she wasn't sure—and he'd promised not to come back to the dispensary.

He told her Narcisso was Alfredo's brother. She took that well although it did surprise her. Then she asked about the lieutenant, saying she'd only caught a glimpse of him as he'd left the building, but that he'd left her with an unfavourable impression.

He smiled. 'You're as perspicacious as the Indians. Lieutenant Honorio was aptly named; he only thinks in terms of God and glory, and I suspect God runs a poor second in that race.'

'And—the other?'

He slumped into his chair. 'Sometimes I wish I'd never heard of anyone named Sanchez, and yet the mayor is a pleasant enough, ineffectual, harmless man, Eloise. No, we will do nothing about this matter. For one thing I'm going out to Avila's estate this afternoon with Ed Lleras of the land reform team. For another, I'm fearful of armed soldiers under a man like Lieutenant Elizondo; I don't want an outraged Sanchez running to Elizondo demanding a search be made for the defiler of his precious daughter.'

She agreed, then thoughtfully said, 'Doctor, if you go see Avila you'll be lucky to get back here in time to take me to dinner.'

He was chagrined. He hadn't kept his word the night before in that matter either. 'Will you excuse me if I'm not back in time?'

She smiled. 'Of course.'

She left and fifteen minutes later, while he was trying to force himself to concentrate upon the now-
useless report, Ed Lleras arrived. In a way it was a relief.
Leonard was weary of Puna, of all the entanglements
with which he was surrounded, and even when he
viewed the battered old American-made jeep vehicle
parked outside and for which Ed Lleras profusely
apologized, he was pleased to be putting it all behind
him at least temporarily.

Lleras knew the way to Jorge Avila's *estancio*.
Narcisso had told him; had even drawn him a map of
sorts and had volunteered to ride along, an offer Lleras
had declined.

The Director was silent for half the trip. He was
obviously on his first important assignment where his
own judgement was to prevail. It would have unnerved
any young official but with the formidable opposition
of a wealthy, influential and powerful landowner up
ahead, Leonard could imagine how Lleras felt.

The countryside changed the farther northwest they
went. The road was poor but the grade was good; it
was simply a matter of indifference and neglect. But
otherwise, there were gigantic trees, underbrush with
flaming red flowers, rich fields and, near the Magdalena River, several little thrifty settlements.

Finally though, as Ed Lleras pointed out on
Narcisso's map, when they began crossing through the
miles of tended fields into the realm of of the landowners, things began to appear as prosperous as anything Leonard had ever seen. Once, they spun past a
gracious, big sprawling adobe *hacienda* which radiated
affluence even though it was barred and locked.

Then they came into the realm of Avila. Here, there

were huge pastures with beautiful horses, fat, dark red cattle, and farther out, immense flat fields of cacao and coffee.

Leonard started Ed Lleras talking by observing that had he been in Avila's place he probably wouldn't have welcomed any scheme which would deprive him of any of this land either.

'But it's not this land,' protested Lleras. 'After all, Doctor, Columbia is a capitalist nation. We know which side of our bread the butter is on. Chase away the men of intelligence and initiative and all that's left are the *campesinos,* and while they are human beings too, they don't contribute much to our national wealth.'

'What land do you want to take from Jorge Avila?'

'Well, he owns five thousand acres up the valley west of Puna. There is another fifteen thousand acres owned by absentee landlords as well. *That* is the land we are going to apportion. It is raw, true, and virgin, but it is level, has ample water, and the soil is rich.'

Leonard began to wonder about something: Avila opposed redistribution. That was common knowledge. But did he really oppose it, or was he simply reacting as any feudal landowner would react to some socialist scheme?

'There,' said Ed Lleras, pointing with one hand towards a long, low *hacienda* with innumerable out-buildings and a large, two-storey barn, which was very unusual in Columbia. 'That is the Avila *estancia*.' In Spanish Lleras added: 'May the Lord go with us!'

By the time they stopped in front of a stone fence separating Jorge Avila's feudal mansion from the yard beyond, Leonard saw crescents of sweat at the armpits of his companion. Poor Ed Lleras.

A swaggering Indian, short, squat, pock-marked and truculent-appearing came over. He was wearing enormous silvered spurs that made music with each step. He looked briefly at Leonard, then fixed muddy black eyes on Ed Lleras, saying nothing at all. It was not a very auspicious welcome, so Leonard piled out to change that. Giving the gaucho glare for glare he curtly said in atrocious Spanish, 'Please inform *el Patron* we are here—at once!'

The cowboy shifted his attention back to Dr Bordon. He'd recognized Lleras, the mestizo, and could no doubt have coped with him, but Leonard Bordon was something else again. One could almost hear the little wheels turning in the man's head as he finally decided caution might indeed be best in this situation. Without a word he turned and swaggered over to the huge *hacienda*, knocked and removed his hat as he waited.

Avila himself opened the door. He saw Leonard and Lleras at once, ignored the cowboy and strode forth into afternoon sunlight. Leonard introduced Lleras, who was awed, obviously, by the size and dark bearded look of *el Patron*.

Avila's gold-flecked eyes studied Lleras coolly. He raised a massive leg, rested one booted foot upon the jeep's bumper and said, 'Well, *Señor* Lleras—now we discuss how this war is to be prosecuted.' Leonard picked out enough of the Spanish words to get the gist of that remark.

'Could we use English?' he inquired. 'Mr Lleras is proficient in it, so are you Mr Avila.'

The tawny eyes switched back. 'Doctor, what did you do with the lad, Roberto Gomez?'

Leonard wasn't prepared for that question. He stood

a moment swiftly groping for the right answer. He never found it. 'He left Puna, Mr Avila.'

'I know that. But where did he go?'

'Why do you want to know?'

The huge *ranchero* straightened up to his full height. 'I have valid reasons. Where?'

'Away. I don't know.'

'Doctor, you had better know. He is my son.'

If someone had jerked the ground from beneath Leonard Bordon he couldn't have felt any more stunned. 'Roberto Gomez—your *son*?'

Avila's eyes brightened with hard humour at Leonard's stammering astonishment. He said, 'Doctor, there are no nightclubs here, no motion picture houses, no television—only that lousy bar at the hotel ... A man takes his diversions as he finds them. Don't act so outraged. You would do the same if you had to live here year in and year out.'

'It's not outrage, I assure you. It's simply surprise.'

'Well, where did my son go, Doctor?'

'Damned if I know, Mr Avila,' said Leonard, looking for a place to sit down and finding one over against the stone wall where a wooden bench stood.

Avila watched this and shrugged, turning his attention back to Eduardo Lleras. '*Señor* Director,' he said in soft, low Spanish. 'You are wasting time here. Go back and get your soldiers. For every man you bring I will field ten.'

Ed Lleras looked for help at Leonard then looked back. 'No soldiers, *Señor*. If I fail, I will fail alone.'

'You will fail, I promise, with or without your soldiers.'

'*Señor*, five thousand worthless acres. Would you have blood on your conscience over *that*?'

Avila slowly shook his head. 'No. Not over that, *Señor*; over the way it is being taken from me. I am old-fashioned enough to believe in the same things San Martín, Sucre, Boliver believed in: Freedom and the right of every man to. . .'

'*Senor*,' broke in Ed Lleras. 'Times have changed. *I* am not responsible for that. Neither are you. But nevertheless they have changed. Please *Señor*—only listen. No one will take your land. They will buy it.'

'And if I don't want to sell, *Señor*, then the machine-guns?'

Leonard said from over in the shade, 'Avila, come off it. You're trying to make something out of nothing and you damned well know it. You could *give* the people that damned land and it wouldn't inhibit your wealth nor your income either, I'm told, one cent.'

'True,' agreed the big man blandly. 'Come inside, it isn't polite even to keep one's enemies standing forever in the heat.'

They followed him. Several curious cowboys stood discreetly in the near distance straining to hear what was being said. They looked crestfallen when the three men entered the house.

Leonard wasn't actually surprised at the richness of the ancient Spanish furniture. He'd rather expected some show of stability and great wealth. Over a fireplace, blackened with age and use, were the raised coats-of-arms of several historic Spanish families. Elsewhere stood stiff, uncomfortable age-blackened chairs and sofas. As Avila waved them to be seated he put a long, slow look upon Ed Lleras.

He said, speaking English, 'Mr Lleras, tell me, where did you go to school?'

'In New York. Later, I got my degree in California.'

Avila smiled thinly. 'I know those places, but of course I am much older. They were different when I was there.'

Ed dropped his crew-cut head like a small bull and bore in again. 'Mr Avila, I'm not here to *take* your land. I'm here to buy it.'

'I said outside, the land is not for sale.'

'Every acre in the world has a price, Mr Avila.'

'All right, Lleras—one hundred U.S. dollars per acre.'

Leonard was tart. 'That's asinine and you know it.'

Avila cocked a tawny eye. 'Doctor. You and I are already enemies.'

Ed Lleras was pale, his forehead beaded with perspiration. 'Mr Avila two *pesos* an acre would be high and we all know it. But if you will give me one month to raise the money I will promise you twenty U.S. dollars an acre.'

Leonard was no less silenced than was Jorge Avila. They sat staring at the younger man. Twenty U.S. dollars was a lot of money; more, in fact, than most Columbians made a month. Multiply it by five thousand and it was a staggering weight of wealth.

Leonard had no idea whether Lleras was authorized to make such an absurd offer but he suspected Lleras was not, so he said, 'Ed, reconsider. I know how you feel but this isn't likely to help anyone and it could completely ruin your career.'

Lleras turned. 'Doctor, when a man knows his principles are right and that fifty years from now everyone else will know it—should he lie down and die because he's afraid to state them, to back them up with his savings and his salary?'

Leonard didn't answer. He thought of his own dilemma in the Sanchez affair and said nothing more.

Chapter Twelve

They left Jorge Avila's *estancio* while there were still sunbeams jumping out all along the road back to Puna but neither of them needed the hour. They argued over Ed Lleras's offer to Avila.

As soon as Ed explained why he'd made that offer Leonard told him he was insane. Lleras had a decent inheritance in Bogotá. That, coupled with a sufficient pledge of his salary, a large mortgage on the home and grounds he'd inherited in Bogotá, plus perhaps a small contribution, should take care of paying off Jorge Avila.

'You are bankrupting yourself,' protested Leonard. 'You will strap yourself with debt until you are middle aged.'

'Doctor, what else can I do? You know what will happen the minute I send the soldiers out to stake out Avila's land.'

'But let's not be so hasty, Ed. Let's take a day or two and see what we can come up with. Perhaps if you can get one of the other owners lined up. . .'

'Doctor, Avila is the leader. Whatever he tells the others, who are mostly not even in the country so he either telegraphs them or writes letters, they will do. No, it is Avila who must succumb first, and it is I who must make certain that he does so.'

They arrived back in town for Leonard to check

97

in at the hotel for a bath, a change of clothing and a stroll to the dispensary. The moment he walked in looking cool, crisp and fresh, Eloise saw him and raised her brow.

He took her into the office and told her two things: One, that George Ritter Avila stubbornly declined to co-operate with the Land Reform Program, and two, that the lad whom he'd given one hundred dollars to —the boy who'd got Mayor Sanchez's daughter into trouble—was Avila's son.

'But he's not married,' she said, blurting it out in surprise.

'You don't really have to be married to have children,' he said ironically. 'It only makes it a little easier on the children. He didn't elaborate, but obviously Roberto Gomez's mother was some local Indian girl or woman. He *did* say that because there were no motion pictures nor televisions he took his diversion where he found it.'

She recovered slowly from the surprise. 'Can you get the boy back?'

'Of course. He's hiding somewhere close by awaiting nightfall to ride out of here with Narcisso Pinzon. And that's the way it's got to be. I suppose, actually, everyone knows who Roberto Gomez is excepting you and I. In any case you can imagine what would happen now if Elfego Sanchez discovers who the lover of his precious Elena is.'

'What?'

'Pandemonium, that's what. Go get your coat and we'll have some dinner. I'm starved.'

She arose. 'I meant to tell you, Doctor: Father Lopez and Mayor Sanchez have been looking for you all afternoon.'

98

'Not together,' he said.

'No.'

'All right. With any luck I can avoid them until the morning. By then at least Gomez will be gone.'

'Not with Narcisso, Doctor. He told me this afternoon he wouldn't be going back to Bogotá for a few days. He wants to be on hand in the event there is trouble with the landowners.'

She left the office to get her coat. He continued to stand behind his table looking increasingly glum. If Narcisso didn't leave . . . There had to be another way to get Roberto Gomez out, and it had to be done tonight before the lad changed his mind and decided to stay in Magdalena Valley to spend his one hundred U.S. dollars, or before something else happened. Leonard had no doubt at all about one thing: Sooner or later—if not within the next day or two then certainly eventually—Elena Sanchez would reveal who her betrayer was.

One of the dark nurses came to say *Señor* Lleras wished to see Dr Bordon. When Ed Lleras walked in he too was crisply clean and presentable again, but his eyes were also troubled.

He said he was sending a truck out this evening with a letter to his banker in Bogotá, and with a watered-down report to his INCORA superior saying it might take a week or two longer to make the land distribution than they'd originally planned.

All Leonard heard was the part about the truck. 'I want you to take a man out on that truck, Ed,' he said.

Lleras nodded indifferently. Evidently he thought it was a patient needing the better facilities available in the capital. Leonard didn't explain this wasn't the case for a very simple reason: If he'd told Lleras his truck would be taking Jorge Avila's son out of Magdalena Valley against the wishes of his father, Lleras—the last person on earth wishing to risk antagonizing Avila—wouldn't have permitted Gomez anywhere near his truck.

Eloise returned and the three of them, after suitable introductions, went outside where the day was fading and several soldiers across the road playing some gambling game in the dust outside the jailhouse had their shinily oiled automatic weapons lined up against the mud wall.

Ed Lleras eyed that scene across the road with a thoughtful expression, then he said softly, 'Sometimes I just don't belong. Sure, I was born in Columbia, but my family sent me to the States for all my schooling. Now,' he nodded at the soldiers, 'scenes like that are straight out of Kafka for me. They're ridiculous.' He looked at Leonard then at Eloise. 'You think *you* are misfits. . .' He walked off in the direction of the INCORA office with his head down.

Leonard told Eloise everything that had happened this day as they made slow progress up towards the hotel. He ended up by saying, 'Now I've got to locate Gomez and get him on Ed Lleras's truck. But how? Of course when Avila found Gomez before, I simply assumed Avila knew his way round. But now Avila wants to know where Gomez is too, so who do I get to find him for me?'

She answered simply. 'Narcisso.'

He stopped in his tracks. 'Of course.' He took her by the shoulders, pulled her close and kissed her squarely on the mouth, thrust her off and started walking again. 'You've hit it squarely on the head, old girl.'

She was startled, obviously, by that kiss, but as he began walking again she did also. Finally, she said, 'I'm delighted to be of help, Doctor, but I don't relish being an "old girl".' She might have mentioned the kiss too.

He was entering the hotel and absently nodded. He hadn't been paying the slightest attention. She knew that when he took her arm to steer her to the dining room instead of the bar as he said, 'Perhaps if you'd order supper for us I could find Narcisso and set him on the trail.'

She clamped her arm against her side as he began withdrawing, in that manner stopping him. 'Doctor, we will eat dinner *then* go find Narcisso. After all it's not even dark out yet, we can't spend more than half an hour eating.'

He let her lead him along.

They had highballs with their dinner. He didn't eat much and in the end she relented—or surrendered, whichever it was—and they returned to the plaza. The first person they met—nearly collided with in fact, was Elfego Sanchez. He looked bad even in the dusk light. He apparently hadn't slept nor eaten since his daughter's disappearance although Leonard smelt liquor on his breath which indicated he hadn't just remained totally in shocked limbo.

Sanchez stopped, sidestepped to avoid collision, then recognized them and said, extending both arms, 'Doctor, still no word. I want you to come round and see my wife. She is lying in bed like a dead person. She won't talk nor eat. She just lies there looking at the ceiling.'

Leonard promised he'd call and got away with tact. He had just seen a shambling, unkempt individual

101

enter the dispensary down the road and even in that poor light had recognized Narcisso Pinzon.

He hustled Eloise along until, near the dispensary doorway, she hauled back. He then explained and she relented. They found Narcisso mildly flirting with the night nurse who promptly faded out into the ward at sight of Eloise and Leonard. Narcisso smiled softly at being caught, gave his thick shoulders a little heave as though to say there was no harm in a little flirting, and removed his old hat to Eloise.

Leonard took them both into his office. He told Narcisso in short, blunt sentences what must be done. He also told Narcisso *why* it had to be done. The Indian puckered his lips in a silent whistle and rolled up his eyes. 'Do you know that boy may have gone back to the Avila *estancio*, Doctor? After all, he is safe there.'

Leonard didn't believe that. 'If he would be safe Narcisso, then why was he skulking around Puna without a penny to his name?'

'Well, of course, I don't know why, Doctor.'

'Nor do I, *amigo*, but I hardly think his father's interest is strongly filial.'

'Eh, *Señor*. . .?'

'I mean I doubt if Avila has fatherly feelings. At least not strong ones. But he'd want to know where the youth was, perhaps out of curiosity. I can't say. I don't actually care, Narcisso. What we've got to do is get the lad on that damned truck tonight. Tell me frankly, Narcisso, can you find him?'

Pinzon had no doubt at all. 'Of course, Doctor. After all, I am known here. I am trusted.' He rolled his eyes to Eloise, considered her briefly then dropped the old hat atop his head. 'I go now. When I have taken care of this business I'll return.' He nodded to Leonard, made a more deliberate bow to Eloise, and left.

Leonard stepped to his rear window—the only one in the little room—and blew out a big breath. To the dark blue night he said, 'I don't know why I should be so upset. It's not really any of my doing.'

Eloise walked over. 'I could point out that but for you it would be taking a different course, Doctor.'

He turned. She was like a fresh flower and he marvelled at that, for even under duress she was still calm and cool. He suddenly recalled the kiss.

'Good heavens,' he muttered and looked quickly away.

That perplexed her. 'Now what?'

'I just remembered something. Most inappropriate, Miss Cutler.'

She smiled at his profile. 'It was very pleasant, really.'

He looked askance at her. 'We probably aren't thinking of the same thing.'

She continued to quietly smile. 'Well, perhaps not, and yet one has a tendency to recall rather astonishing events.'

'I kissed you, Miss Cutler. You must understand that in the excitement of the moment. . .'

Her smile lingered as she said, 'That's not very flattering Doctor.'

He floundered. 'Well, it was gratitude for thinking of Narcisso. I was completely blank on what to do about locating Gomez. You came to my rescue.'

'Efficient Eloise, Doctor, that's what they used to call me at home. Good old reliable, efficient Eloise.'

He detected the irony and looked squarely at her. 'No, I would never limit my admiration to your efficiency, Miss Cutler. But on the other hand, with the impressions you've given me—you wouldn't be interested in having me admire you for anything else, I'm sure.'

She stood facing him, very close and very lovely, the perfect column of her neck showing a shadowy V where a gentle pulse beat. 'Don't be so sure of that, Doctor,' she said.

He saw the colour mounting into her cheeks, saw the heavy, languid fulness of her beautiful mouth and the quiet softness of her eyes. He said exactly what he was thinking. 'You are the most thoroughly lovely woman I've ever known.'

She was up against him, his arms were around her. He found her lips warmly receptive. It surprised him but more than that, it made him feel slightly giddy, slightly breathless as though he'd just run a long mile.

She returned his kiss with a lingering tenderness that revealed to him a part of her character he'd never suspected. She was *all* woman, not just part woman as he'd been led to surmise.

He said in a low whisper, 'My God, Miss Cutler.'

It made her laugh, but a brisk knock on the door broke them apart so swiftly her laugh was cut short. He looked near panic for one second, then recovered, turned and crossed to the door. Before admitting whoever was out there he looked back. She was watching him. She roguishly dropped one eyelid and raised it. He waited a moment, returned the wink, then flung open the door.

Father Eusebio Lopez was standing out there nervously clutching the arm of a very slight although well-rounded girl who had a veil over her face and a heavy *mantilla* over her head and shoulders. Lopez almost shoved the girl into the office, jumped in himself and swiftly closed the door.

Leonard discreetly shot the bolt locking the door, then he woodenly gestured towards chairs. He knew who the girl was without seeing her face nor hearing her name. Elena Sanchez!

Chapter Thirteen

The girl had been weeping, but then Leonard hardly expected much else. Her face was puffy and only because she was quite young did it have any prettiness at all.

The features were weak, soft and round, the eyes light brown like the hair, the mouth and chin pliant. Leonard looked at Eloise. She returned his gaze without comment but she moved across the room to take a chair nearer the girl.

Father Lopez said 'I apologize for doing this, Doctor, for bringing her here, but her father is making enquiries everywhere. People are beginning to talk. At least a dozen have stopped me just to ask what I think should be done.'

Leonard felt like asking what Lopez expected him to do. The reason he didn't ask was because he knew exactly what the answer would be. To kill time while he came to some decision, he went over to the girl, stood gazing at her a moment, then spoke softly while he made a very cursory examination. There was something—he never could define it exactly—that struck him wrong. He didn't mention it however and paced back behind his table.

'If you leave her here,' he told the priest, 'she'll be recognized at once.'

'Doctor,' said Lopez desperately, 'I can't continue

to hide them in the cathedral!'

Leonard stared. 'Them. . .?'

'Yes. The boy came seeking sanctuary until Pinzon leaves tonight.'

Eloise looked surprised. 'Father, you have Roberto Gomez at the church?'

Lopez nodded, then looked reproachfully at Leonard. 'I thought his identity was our secret,' he said.

Leonard turned brisk. 'Father; I have no secrets from Nurse Cutler.' He looked over but Eloise was already arising. She nodded at him without either of them saying a word, unlocked the door and passed out into the reception room beyond. None of them had anything to say until she'd closed the door then Leonard looked at his wristwatch. It was almost nine o'clock. He didn't know what time Ed Lleras would be sending his lorry out.

He decided, with Eloise seeking Narcisso, and Pinzon seeking Gomez, there really wasn't much he could do, personally, now. Whatever happened out there in the darkness would be in other hands.

He turned back to studying the Sanchez girl. That earlier hunch returned. He told Father Lopez to keep her in the office while he went after some things. He didn't explain what it was he was going after, but when he had them from the operating room he paused in the silence of the darkened little room to think ahead for a moment.

Of one thing he was certain: Elfego Sanchez was very soon now going to find his wayward daughter. After all, Puna just wasn't London or Birmingham; there was no possible way to secrete a living person indefinitely in a place as insular and close-knit as Magadalena Valley.

He returned to the Office, pricked Elena's finger for a blood sample, took her pulse, asked a few questions, then stood a moment with his back to them both while he gazed out into the starry, clear night. When he turned back eventually he told Father Lopez there just was no way for Elena Sanchez to stay at the dispensary; he must take her back to the cathedral and hide for another day at the very least.

Lopez was anguished. 'But we must *do* something, Doctor. This condition is at best only temporary.'

Leonard concurred. He said he had a house-call to make and promised to come round to the church in the morning. He then took Father Lopez and Elena Sanchez out through the darkened dispensary to a small rear doorway and got rid of them. For a moment afterwards he stood in darkness running several conflicting things through his mind before returning to the office, snatching up his little black bag and rushing forth into the night bound for the residence of Mayor Sanchez.

He hadn't been able to test the blood sample from the girl but he had a gnawing doubt anyway. He'd have Eloise do the laboratory work when she returned but in the interim he wanted to see *Señora* Sanchez.

He saw her. Elfego admitted him to the darkened little house with its small but elegant courtyard. With scarceley more than a sad greeting the mayor took Leonard to his wife's bedroom.

There were two candles burning. There was also an electric lamp but no one had turned it on. Neither did Leonard; he recognised the candles as votary lights and respected the faith of whoever had lit them. Anyway, for what he had to do he didn't need much more light.

He told the mayor's wife who he was. She looked into his face with perfectly dry and blank eyes, then looked back at the ceiling again. Her husband hovered near the doorway gripping his hands together.

Leonard asked *Señora* Sanchez about the birthing of her only child. She didn't answer but Elfego did. He said his wife had been very ill much of the time; that he'd taken her to Bogotá several times and the doctors there had said something about her blood being wrong. Elfego had not understood very much of what he'd been told but he remembered being warned against additional children unless he was willing to move to Bogotá where expert aid was available.

'It was the blood,' he told Leonard. 'It was bad for the child.'

Leonard had his answer; that was all he'd come for. He'd suspected the same negative factor in Elena but couldn't be sure until Elena's blood had been through the laboratory tests. Now he was certain, but all any of this meant was that if Elena went ahead and had her child, it would be born maimed. If not in body then in mind.

He closed his bag, studied the wasted, slack face on the bed, leaned over and whispered in poor Spanish for *el Señora* to stop worrying; that her child would be returned to her shortly. Then, with those dead eyes coming down off the ceiling to gaze at him wonderingly, he smiled, patted the woman's folded hands and arose.

Elfego guided him through the gloomy, dark house back into the elegant little courtyard. There, the mayor said, 'It is no use, Doctor. You saw how she is. I have tried telling her the same thing and it is no use.'

There was really nothing more to be said. Leonard

stood in silence for a while, then left. Sanchez went as far as the front gate and watched his guest move off through the gloom.

At the dispensary Eloise was impatiently pacing. She told him at once that she'd located Narcisso and he'd gone to the church for Roberto Gomez. She also said Ed Lleras was ready to start the truck back. He was enormously relieved, for even though he had no clue yet as to where all this would end, at least he had made certain of one thing: There would be no honour-killing of Gomez by Elfego Sanchez, and the results of such a killing—Avila storming Puna to avenge his dead son—had also been averted.

He gave Eloise the blood sample, told her quietly about his earlier thoughts, explained what he'd suspected, and how he'd confirmed it, at least to his own satisfaction, by visiting Elena's mother, then urged her to make the laboratory tests immediately so they'd be certain whether Elena was in fact an RH Negative type.

Eloise left him.

He dropped down at the table feeling weary. It had been a long, disagreeable day. He wasn't tired as much as completely drained dry of energy. The dinner and highball had helped.

He considered working on the blasted report but its importance had been superseded by events lately, and furthermore, now that the decision had been made to establish a hospital at Puna, the report wasn't essential anyway, except to the bureaucrats who needed something to support their previous claims.

Narcisso Pinzon came by an hour later to say that Lleras's INCORA lorry had departed—with Roberto Gomez aboard. Then Narcisso dropped into a chair, shook his head and related to Leonard the gist of a long, rambling conversation he'd had with Roberto.

Leonard inquired as to whether or not Narcisso knew Jorge Avila was Roberto's father. Narcisso shrugged. He had known, he said. 'It was generally known, Doctor, but if you are shocked you shouldn't be. After all, *Señor* Avila is a powerful man.

Leonard didn't get the connexion, but then he doubted, after some reflection, whether he'd ever completely understand these people, if he lived among them a lifetime.

'Well, it is done anyway,' he muttered, and yawned. 'And I suppose Roberto told you why he was leaving?'

Narcisso smiled gently. 'With your one hundred dollars. Yes, he told me. But it was too much money. Half, even a third as much, would have been sufficient. After all, Roberto can go all the way to Mexico on a hundred dollars.'

Narcisso said that as though Mexico were the end of the earth. To a native of Columbia it *was*.

One thing still rankled. Leonard mentioned it. 'Why wasn't Avila more concerned—or do I do him an injustice; I don't understand all this, Narcisso.'

The Indian's dark eyes continued thoughtful as he considered the darkness beyond Leonard's window. window. 'Doctor, I tell you something: When we first rode together over the Cordillera, I asked that you try to understand.'

'I remember.'

'Well, do you know how long Columbians have been without decency? Since long before anyone can recall. But the feelings and needs were always there. Doctor, I doubt very much if more than one half of my people were born when their parents were married by a priest.

It just hasn't always been possible. But I've seen a lot of the other kind, and I tell you something; my people are no worse. In most cases they aren't even nearly as bad. So—the priest's blessing hasn't improved the world very much has it?'

Leonard smiled. 'No, I'm afraid it hasn't. But why would Avila. . .?'

'*Quien sabe,* Doctor? Who knows why a strong man acts as he does? *Señor* Avila was interested, maybe, otherwise he wouldn't have asked you about the boy. But who can say how much else a father feels?'

Leonard had to abandon that topic. Neither he nor Narcisso Pinzon knew any more after talking it over than either of them had known before.

Eloise came in, saw Narcisso and hesitated. Leonard urged her to come right out with whatever she had to say. Her words were blunt.

'If the girl has the baby she'll have to be taken to Bogotá at once to be under proper care. She definitely has the wrong type blood for a normal child to be born to her.'

Leonard looked at Eloise a long time. How did they smuggle Elena Sanchez out of Magdalena Valley when everyone was searching high and low? Of course a helicopter would do very nicely, but there were no helicopters and no way to discreetly acquire one.

'Well,' he said. 'You are resourceful, Narcisso; what do you think?'

Pinzon only sadly shook his head. 'There would be no way that I know of. Even if she were stolen out of Puna in the dead of night, someone on the road would surely see her riding in a car.' He looked soberly at Leonard. 'But if you wish I will try it.'

'And what will happen if you are caught?'

Narcisso didn't answer, he placed a cocked right hand against his own temple and pulled an imaginary trigger. It was graphically illustrative.

'Forget it,' said Leonard, arising. 'We'll have to come up with something else. Perhaps tell her father exactly what has happened, now that Roberto is out of the way, and impress upon him the importance of taking her to Bogotá himself At any rate, let's all go home and sleep on it.'

Narcisso left first. Eloise had to show Leonard her written analysis. Not that he doubted her at all but this was customary; they were both too well-trained to take needless short-cuts.

He tossed the analysis on the table beside his unfinished report and gazed at her. 'What do you think now?' he asked.

'I don't see any alternative but to tell Mayor Sanchez. There is a little room for delay. She's only been pregnant a short while. But too much delay can complicate things.'

He uttered a short, abrasive laugh. 'Complicate things? Eloise, the minute we tell Sanchez the complications are just going to begin. He'll know Father Lopez hid her. He'll probably know what you and I didn't know—that Roberto was the son of Avila.' Leonard threw up his hands. 'I don't see anything but additional complications *ad infinitum.*'

She remained perfectly calm. 'True. But that is how it's all going to come out in the end anyway; you knew that, Doctor, so did I when I volunteered to help.'

He studied her a moment. She had an almost uncanny way of always appearing crisply cool, fresh and capable. He knew how *he* felt—tired—and he also knew he looked it. He sat on the edge of the table no

113

longer so anxious to leave.

'Tell me something, Nurse,' he said. 'Were you taught to always be loyal to your physicians?'

'Always,' she replied, looking him squarely in the eye. 'But only loyal, Doctor. Nothing more.'

'That's gratifying, Miss Cutler. Then that kiss. . .'

'I meant it. I'd mean it again.'

He stood up. She was tall for a woman but she was still half a head shorter than he was. He walked over and said, 'Prove it.'

She did. She stepped up, leaned and kissed him in that same, softly thrilling, lingering way. He felt for her, held her close and when she put her cheek against the side of his head he whispered, 'This is the most unnerving thing that ever happened to me.'

'And me,' she said quietly. 'But, I've seen it coming.'

'You have? But it's probably simply that you've been out here so long without compatible companionship.'

She pulled back to look at him. 'Do you believe that?'

He didn't know. He said, 'It was just a suggestion.'

She reached up to trace the outline of his lips with a delicate fingertip. 'No, Doctor, it's not propinquity. Nor is it some passionate hunger. It's just that after all the waiting the right man has finally arrived. And of all places in this god-forsaken Andean valley with enough trouble on all sides to prevent any reasonable person from thinking of romance—unless it *was* the right person.'

He dropped his head. She lifted her face. That time the kiss was as gentle as the touch of a feather, but it left his heart beating furiously and when she drew away she lay limp in his arms. It had affected her the same way.

114

Chapter Fourteen

The report came at eleven the following morning. It couldn't have come any sooner because no one came down off the mountain nor went driving up along it. The road had broken loose up there, sliding a thousand feet downhill. It hadn't roared down into the chasm but had freakishly slid only as far as an outcropping of grey granite.

A number of people got horses or old automobiles and went up to see. Horses were better because there weren't any places for autos to turn round up there.

The entire affair was a diversion. In most quarters a welcome diversion from the sameness of everyday existence. As far as Leonard was concerned, he had his supplies, Roberto Gomez had passed over the road a long while earlier, and with just one exception he didn't care that it would require at least two weeks by the best local estimates before the road could be repaired and made traversable again.

'The girl,' he told Eloise. 'She will need prompt medical aid providing her condition is sufficiently advanced. I could tell very little last night. Perhaps I should have insisted upon giving her a thorough examination. The reason I didn't was because if I had Father Lopez would have interpreted it as sympathetic interest.'

Eloise said she would go to the church and look at

the girl. They agreed between them it would be better if she went; too many visits by the doctor to the cathedral might arouse curiosity.

After Eloise departed Leonard made two trips into the ward. One was to ascertain whether Alfredo Pinzon was sufficiently recovered to be discharged, which he was, and the other visit was to Felicidad and her infant.

The girl was miraculously changed. She smiled, showing small white teeth. There was colour in her cheeks and a definite hint of plumpness in her child. It was rather amazing, considering the short length of time she'd been at the dispensary.

She told Leonard in carefully rehearsed English she was forever grateful for what he'd done for them. She would now name her son after him.

He took one of the little nurses aside, asked about the child, was told it responded well, then gave the nurse some money to go out and buy a crisp white dress for Felicidad, and a little blue one for her son.

Otherwise, there were the usual patients with uninteresting cases, all of them non-committal in the Indian way, their obsidian eyes following Leonard's each move.

Ed Lleras came round as Leonard was finishing his rounds. They met in the reception room, Lleras coming in from the road, Leonard heading on across to his office. He took Lleras in with him, got him a chair and removed the white ward-coat and hung it up.

Lleras asked if Leonard had heard of the landslide. He said it would hinder the work of INCORA, but that Lleras planned no changes because of that.

He'd sent his team out into the country in the army lorries to post notices. 'The people can see how they

116

must come to Puna and fill out a form, then receive their allotment of land.'

'Ed, most of them can't read.'

Lleras was prepared. 'I have amplifiers atop the lorries attached to the intercom units inside. The team members will explain over and over again what is required to qualify for the land at every village and hovel.'

Lleras smiled. He was a very sincere young man, likeable and honest and pleasant. Leonard wanted him to succeed. He said, 'Ed, how can you go ahead when you aren't sure yet that you have the land to distribute?'

'I have the land, Doctor. I certainly wouldn't have said it yesterday in front of *Señor* Avila, but his land and all the other land was expropriated by the government before I left Bogotá. I am empowered to give grant deeds to each family for their twelve and a half acres.'

Leonard digested that and didn't much care for it. What kind of government arbitrarily took away its people's property; not a very good one he was afraid.

As though Ed Lleras understood he said, 'Doctor, there is unrest. What happened here a few years back can very definitely occur again. The Land Reform Program can't wait.'

'Jorge Avila might think otherwise. Ed, suppose he decides not to accept your offer to buy the land?'

Lleras nodded. 'I didn't sleep much last night thinking about what I did. But I still believe I did exactly right. He'll accept. Didn't you see the cupidity in his face when I made the offer yesterday?'

'I saw something,' agreed Leonard, 'but it seemed more like incredulity to me than cupidity very much. In the first place it wasn't a whole lot of money by his standards, in the second place I'm told on good authority that George Ritter Avila is very rich—unlikely to need more money.'

'Of course,' said Ed Lleras, 'if all else fails, then I have those troops out there. But of course that will end with Avila's death—either fighting or before a firing squad or in battle, and it also means I'll be replaced on my first assignment.'

'What day have you set for the *campesinos* to arrive in Puna to fill out the land forms?'

Ed Lleras raised his boyish face. 'Tomorrow, Doctor.'

Leonard was shocked. 'Tomorrow? Whatever possessed you, Ed? You should have waited at least a week.'

'I couldn't. Last night I was informed by telephone my Magdalena project is lagging far behind all the other projects. Doctor, I'm damned if I do and damned if I don't. If I bring war I'll be replaced for not being able to cajole Avila, and if I could through some miracle bring him round, I'd still have wasted too much time. For that matter I set tomorrow as the day for filing on the land.'

Ed rose, gazed steadily at Leonard a moment, then showed that boyish, infectious smile again, but it was more wistful this time and less effervescent. Leonard went to the door with Lleras. There were occasions —they did not occur in *everyone's* lifetime—when a youth had to become a man overnight. This was such a time for likeable Ed Lleras and Leonard felt sorry for him.

After Lleras left Eloise returned. They went to the hotel for a bite to eat. She said the Sanchez girl was farther along than the girl herself knew. Of course the implication behind those words was plain enough without Eloise spelling it out. He made his decision.

'After luncheon, Eloise, you go back to the dispensary and get ready.'

'Where are you going?'

'To see Father Lopez first and have him bring the girl to you to be scrubbed and prepared. Then to the Sanchez house.'

Eloise stiffened in her chair across from him. He did not at once notice, but eventually looking up at her, he saw the way she was gazing over his shoulder. He turned and saw George Ritter Avila coming across the room towards their table.

Leonard said, 'Steady on,' and returned to his luncheon.

Avila took a chair from a nearby table, spun it and dropped astraddle with his thick arms hooked over the top. He scarcely glanced at Eloise and when he spoke to Leonard his voice was pleasant enough.

'Doctor, a very odd thing has happened. Last night Roberto went out of the valley in one of those government lorries.'

Leonard raised his head slightly, touched lips with a napkin signifying he'd finished the meal, then turned the chair so he was facing Avila. He knew about what could come out of this meeting. What he had to ascertain now, was which of the unpleasant alternatives would Avila choose. He waited, unwilling to comment for obvious reasons. Avila smiled, his tawny eyes drawn out narrow.

'You have nothing to say about that. Well, I can appreciate that you are not a liar.'

Leonard still sat silent. He *wasn't* a liar and he wasn't going to be made one by this man. They exchanged a long look. Eloise, uncomfortable during this interim, arose saying she really should get back to the dispensary. She cast a meaningful look at Leonard as he arose along with Avila. Leonard understood what that look meant.

'I'll be along,' he said.

As she walked away, Avila watching, Leonard reseated himself. Avila, bringing his attention back again, straddled the chair with a grunt. 'Lleras,' he mused, 'is one of those very sincere, idealistic young men. He also happens to be a fool. Did you tell him he was going to pauperize himself making that offer for the land?'

'I used a different word,' said Leonard. 'I told him he'd bankrupt himself.'

Avila gently inclined his head. 'A better word no doubt. My English is rusty.'

'So is your heart if you make him keep his word.'

Avila kept studying Leonard a moment, his narrowed tawny eyes thoughtful. 'Tell me why you gave my son a hundred dollars to leave and never return.'

The bluntness was something Leonard understood. What he had trouble keeping up with was the way Jorge Avila jumped from one topic to another without warning.

'To keep him from getting killed.'

Avila's eyes widened slightly. 'Explain,' he said.

'Someday, perhaps. Not now.'

'Doctor, I can wring it out of you.'

'No, you can't. I said once before if you'd like to try come right ahead.'

Avila's brows furrowed. He evidently was mildly puzzled. Dr Bordon should have quailed. Avila was taller, much heavier, and obviously capable. But this slim, lanky Englishman wasn't the least bit fearful. 'Maybe,' he drawled, 'You are the "dead hero" type, Doctor. Maybe you are simply foolish.'

'And maybe,' said Leonard, 'there is a third alternative. You can find out easily enough if you really desire to.'

Avila shook his large head as though warding off a minor annoyance. He jumped topics again. 'You wonder how I know you gave Roberto a hundred Yanqui dollars and sent him out of the valley.'

Leonard conceded his curiosity was piqued. Avila fished a paper from a pocket and spread it upon the table between them. Leonard could pick out his own name and one or two significant words. It was the signature that interested him. 'Alfredo Pinzon.'

He sighed. Narcisso must have leaked the information to Alfredo, his brother. He shook his head wearily and looked up. Avila was watching him. Leonard said, 'Tell me something; you don't really care about Roberto, so what difference does all this make to you?'

'I care about the lad, Doctor. I just don't believe in pampering boys. Girls—a little. Boys, never. Raise them tough, hard, resourceful and they grow into good strong men.'

'Ethics, *Señor*, honour, integrity, decency?'

Avilo straightened up. 'What did he do, Doctor? Who would have—' Avila suddenly stopped speaking and sat perfectly still. Clearly, a thought struck him with the force of a great physical blow. After a while he said in a very low tone, 'The Sanchez girl. She ran away. I heard about that a day or two ago. Roberto used to go see her a lot. Doctor. . .?'

Leonard simply nodded once.

Jorge Avila slowly resumed his former hunched

position across the back of the chair. He didn't remove his eyes from Leonard for a long while, then he growled for a waiter and called for a bottle of whisky and two glasses. For a tough, cynical *ranchero*, Jorge Avila was shaken.

Finally he said, 'I understand now. Sanchez ... You thought Elfego Sanchez would shoot Roberto.'

'Wouldn't he?'

Avila waited until the bottle and glasses came, poured two full shots and lifted his before speaking again. 'It is customary, yes. But I doubt that Sanchez would do that to anyone connected with me.'

'Señor, blood is thicker than water—or bought loyalty.'

'Drink,' said Avila, pouring a second shot. Leonard drank the first one. It burnt all the way down. The liquor was Mexican *tequila*, as tart as acid and twice as potent. He placed one hand palm-down over the glass refusing the second shot.

Avila gave a great sigh after the second shot and hung morosely in his chair staring at their empty glasses. 'Well,' he ultimately growled, 'A boy becomes a man.'

'What kind of a man, *Señor*?'

'Yes,' muttered the rich ranchero. 'What kind of a man. All right; I'll pay you back the hundred Yanqui dollars.'

'No, you won't. I wouldn't touch any of your money with a long pole.'

Avila was stung and showed it. Leonard bored in with another quiet, telling remark.

'As for Sanchez—I'm trying to prevent his knowing. I'm not at all sure it can be done. If it can't, then at least I want to prevent everyone else from knowing.

Why rub a father's nose in it because his daughter was weak and her lover was unscrupulous?'

'You are being reckless, Doctor, in your choice of words.'

'Not as reckless as you've been—in other matters,' said Leonard arising. 'I've got to get back to the dispensary. Excuse me, please.'

He walked away expecting to be roared at. It didn't happen. He also expected to be followed. That didn't happen either.

Chapter Fifteen

He didn't go directly to the dispensary nor had that been his intention, instead he went to the huge old gloomy cathedral with its massive adobe walls four feet thick and its faint scent of incense. Father Lopez met him near the inner courtyard as though expecting him —which of course he was. Without more than a sombre nod the priest led him out back where that wonderfully cool and uniformly shady, great long patio was. They seated themselves away from the possibility of being overheard in their conversation.

Leonard felt the *tequila* and mopped his face. 'Send the girl to Miss Cutler at the dispensary,' he said.

Father Lopez nodded. 'Miss Cutler came and got her, Doctor, about a half hour ago.'

'In that case I'm wasting time here.'

'Wait, Doctor. There is something else.'

'Of course. Her parents,' Leonard arose looking sceptically at the priest. 'I'll keep you out of it if I can.' Bleakly smiling he said, 'Father, this is your little mess yet I find myself the primary villain. I will protect you as I've tried to protect Roberto Gomez. Who, might I ask, is going to protect me?'

'Are you decided then about the unborn one?'

Leonard gazed out where a golden sun lay, burnishing some far-away mountains the colour of Aztec

gold. 'I had that decision made for me, Father. In lay
terms—the girl cannot have a normal child without
highly sophisticated medical help. We don't have the
facilities at the Puna dispensary.'

'Do they have those facilities in Bogotá?'

Leonard looked at Lopez steadily. 'Yes. And it will
take half a month or longer to repair the road, Father,
so how do we get her to Bogotá?'

Eusebio Lopez comprehended slowly and sighed,
clasping his hands together. He arose. 'I will go with
you.'

Leonard wasn't going back to the dispensary just yet.
Nevertheless he turned over in his mind the advantage
of taking the priest with him to the Sanchez home.
He decided to do it.

'Come along then, Father. I'm going to tell Elfego
Sanchez and his wife their daughter is safe at the
dispensary but she needs a minor operation.'

Father Lopez stood like carved, lark stone. 'They
will of cousse ask where she has been hiding.'

Leonard looked at the younger man. 'Father, a little
while ago I was placed in the position where I had to
lie or be truthful. I didn't like the situation. Now it's
your bloody turn. Come along.'

They left the cathedral side by side. A flat-faced
Indian woman of indeterminate age appeared silently
in a doorway to watch them depart. She was Eusebio
Lopez's housekeeper.

The day was well advanced as they trudged together
around the plaza and down the little roadway leading
to the Sanchez residence. They said little; obviously
Father Lopez's thoughts were upon his rather shaky
position in the Sanchez affair. He had without any
doubt risked de-frocking simply by harbouring the

runaway girl. Worse—infinitely worse—he'd advocated abortion.

Of course he hadn't done that lightly. Leonard saw the strain in his face and imagined how it must have torn him internally. Once, as they walked along, Leonard said, 'Father, every man has a god of some kind in his heart. I think your god is a modern spirit in a backward place. Of course I agree with your thinking but it seems quite doubtful to me that other priests would.'

Lopez shuffled along, silent. Just before they reached the Sanchez house he looked up. 'There are many priests who take a deeper social cognizance of the changing human field, Doctor. But that merely makes us liable to charges of heresy among the older priests. I did a foolish thing. It was not necessary for me to become so involved.'

'You told me when I first came here the church, too, had failed these people. Father, I think in the Sanchez affair you've proven that the church *is* involved. Not just in ritual but in living.'

Lopez smiled a weak little grin. 'I am grateful, Doctor, although yeour defence won't be enough if I'm called to explain later on.'

The Sanchez house was cool, gloomy, and still. Even the elegant little courtyard, completely walled off from the roadway and profusely alive with birds and flowering bushes, seemed hushed as Leonard crossed it to rap upon the yonder door.

Elfego came, looking thin and dull. He saw the priest and gripped the edge of the door, fear starting swiftly into his eyes. 'Something has happened,' he groaned.

Leonard drew him outside, closed the door, led him

to a shady bench and pushed him down. There was a time for tact, for compassion, for great kindness. This, despite Sanchez's obvious condition, was not that time, nor, under the circumstances, was Leonard Bordon the man for those murmured Latin amenities.

He said shortly, '*Señor*, your daughter is at the dispensary.'

Sanchez's head rolled on his neck as he raised a grey face, mute and fearful.

'She is well. That is, as far as her physical condition is concerned, she is as well as when she ran off.'

Incredulity slowly came into the dull eyes. 'She is —well. . .?'

'Listen to me, *Señor*: What I am going to tell you is not a pretty story but so far only half a dozen or so people know it. It is my intention to see that it doesn't become general knowledge. I need your help. I also need your co-operation.'

Sanchez's colour was returning. Patently, he didn't understand all that Leonard was saying but what appeared most important to him was the knowledge that his only child was not dead as he evidently had assumed. He flung out his arms.

'Anything, Doctor. Anything at all.'

Leonard was saturnine. 'I wonder if you'll still say that five minutes from now. *Señor*, your daughter must have an operation.'

'She is ill?' Sanchez's arms dropped, his shoulders sagged. 'She may die?'

'She won't die but she needs this operation. I require your permission on a signed piece of paper since she is under the age of consent. Will you give it?'

'Of course.' Sanchez looked at the priest. 'Father. . .?'

Lopez moved to lay a dark hand upon the older

man's shoulder. 'The doctor is perfectly right, Elfego.'

Sanchez looked from one to the other of them. 'This illness—what is it called?'

Leonard took a big breath. 'Pregnancy.'

Sanchez blanched as though he'd been struck. His mouth opened and closed. He half arose but Father Lopez's hand pressed him back down. Finally, Elfego looked swiftly towards the closed front door. There was no one there. He loosened and slumped on the bench.

There might have been a more prolonged way; some more diplomatic manner of bringing the truth out. But however it was done the shock would always be the same and Leonard was not given to flowery speeches anyway. He had this very unpleasant job to do and he did it. Now, it was out in the open.

Sanchez reacted somewhat as Leonard had expected, but without the Latin fire. 'Who?' he asked. 'Who did this?'

'Your daughter,' said Leonard.

'No, *Señor*. What man?'

Leonard shook his head grimly. 'The man is not important. Since no force was involved, Elfego, you can blame nature, instinct, anything you wish—but you cannot blame a man.'

Father Lopez concurred. 'For now anyway,' he said, 'think of Elena. Later on we will discuss other things. What, for example, will you tell your wife?'

That was a shrewd blow by the priest. Elfego's eyes turned anxious. 'What *shall* I tell her?' he asked Lopez. 'What does a husband say to his wife when their only child has sinned against. . .?'

Leonard brutally cut the conversation back to his particular interest in the matter. 'Come to the dispensary with us,' he said. 'See Elena, sign the papers

128

I'll draw up, then you can think over what to tell your wife. Take plenty of time, Mr Sanchez, plenty of time. Whatever you decide is going to be between the three of you for the rest of your lives.'

Sanchez arose mechanically looking again at the closed door. 'Wait,' he said, and turned, but Father Lopez was quicker. Holding to Sanchez's arm he detained him.

'Say nothing now. Wait until you've seen Elena and can be here with your wife. Don't tell her, then go off with us. When she hears the girl is safe she'll need someone with her.'

Leonard watched Lopez's dark face and agreed. His personal sympathy went out to the youthful priest. If he could have cursed anyone for putting them all into this untenable situation it would have been the nature that gives the young such strong hungers. But he had no time to blame anyone or anything. He jerked his head and turned to pass out of the courtyard into the dusty roadway.

They passed a number of people on the way to the dispensary including Ed Lleras in khaki and laced boots, and Narcisso Pinzon. The former smiled and nodded, the latter simply looked then looked away.

Eloise was waiting. She didn't have to be told that Sanchez knew the secret as she took him to his daughter in a private little examination room. Father Lopez went along. Eloise returned to Leonard's office, closed the door with her back to it and stared.

He was standing by the window. Without turning he said, 'I was just thinking—there should be some way for a man to at least suspect what he is going to encounter in this life, so he could have some previous thoughts and make the right decisions.'

'You've made the right ones every time so far,' she replied, crossing slowly to stand beside him gazing out into the golden daylight. 'I have marvelled at that, Doctor.'

He turned, smiling. 'I didn't just mean Miss Sanchez, I also meant—well—you.'

She waited, watching his eyes and lips. 'There is more,' she prompted.

'It's not very complicated, Miss Cutler. I'm in love.'

Her eyes turned soft, turned tender. 'Isn't that a coincidence. So am I.'

He stood without moving. 'Well, *that's* mainly what I was thinking of when I said it would help if a person had some idea what lay ahead.'

'It wouldn't make any difference, Doctor. I've lain awake the past few nights thinking of it all. There would be little we'd change if we'd had some forewarning. At least *I* wouldn't change any of it.'

'In that case have you considered the possibility of marriage in those sleepless hours?'

She smiled gently. 'I've never considered anything else with as much trepidation, Doctor.'

'Any particular time, Nurse?'

She laughed in a throaty, soft manner. 'Do you have any aversion to being married by a priest instead of a minister?'

'None.'

'Then—would tomorrow evening be too soon?'

He looked at her with a broad twinkle. 'You have just proposed to me, Nurse Cutler.'

'I also thought about that, Dr Bordon, because it's appeared to me unless I took the bull by the horns, if you'll pardon the cliché, you might quite forget to ask.'

He reached. She leaned a little. Her heavy lips were

loose and soft as velvet when he touched them. Neither of them were children. Neither was without full knowledge of what marriage and love implied. Because of this essential maturity they didn't have to explode with the fire, the hunger and want of youth. Their kiss was a subtle blending of need as much as want, of complete and dedicated compatibility as much as passion.

She finally eased back. 'The tears and recriminations must be over by now with the Sanchezes, Leonard. Shouldn't we go?'

'About this operation,' he began, but she lay a finger over his lips.

'There is no other way.'

'The road isn't really a proper barrier you realise.'

'Of course. We could telephone out, request an army helicopter. But that's not the primary consideration, is it?'

He shook his head and, taking her by the hand, left the office.

There were many aspects of what he was now going to do which might in other places be considered thoroughly unorthodox, even unethical. But this was not entirely clear, but such is the way with ingrained, outmoded morality.

Chapter Sixteen

The scene in that small examination room was one of heart-rending anguish, but although Leonard could sympathize, he was perfectly content to have Father Lopez lead the tearful father away after Eloise had shown Sanchez where to sign the release form.

As for the surgery itself, there was nothing at all difficult nor particularly perilous about it. The entire undertaking was satisfactorily concluded in short order and Elena Sanchez was taken into another isolated little room for her initial rest and recovery. When Leonard met Eloise later she complimented him. He thanked her, of course, but as he said, it wasn't a bit of work he took any pride in.

They remained in the ward for a short while looking at other patients. Neither of them was anxious to go down to Leonard's office and listen to the loud lamentations of Elfego Sanchez, nor the pontifical solemnity of Father Lopez.

They visited with Felicidad and her infant son. The baby was remarkably improved considering the relatively short length of time he'd been at the dispensary. Felicidad's shiny black hair was growing back thick as ever, her piquant face was rounder, fuller, and there was a shy sparkle in her eye.

She had a fine white dress, starched. Her little son had a blue suit. Felicidad helped the other nurses.

They liked her and as Eloise said when they walked away, this was very probably the first real home Felicidad had ever known. She felt she belonged here, was important to the dispensary, meant something to the people—well and ill—but primarily to the ill, and she was correct, for with the dispensary being chronically short-handed, she was a very welcome addition to staff.

Leonard took the long view. 'I leave in one more month. You leave a little sooner. What becomes of Felicidad and her baby, then?'

'Others will come to replace us.'

'Certainly, but what guarantee do we have they won't decide in view of Felicidad's past they won't want her around?'

Eloise looked down as she said, 'I hardly think anyone would be that, cruel, Leonard.'

She knew people *could* be that cruel and so did he. He took her hand and led her out behind the dispensary where the raw land began. He'd once had some notion of getting flowers to grow back there, but it had been a very brief and illusory notion; he hadn't had time to do anything about. He was convinced as he stood in that quiet, secluded place, he never would do anything about it either.

'It's an awesome land,' she said, clinging to him. 'The first thing I noticed was the silence. There are people all around you—yet there's silence. It's a bit unnerving.'

He'd noticed too. It was so terribly different from anything he'd ever before experienced. Two things stood out: The timelessness of the land, the environment, the people. The other thing was a cruelty inherent in the Indian soul that was completely con-

133

tradicted by Indian virtues. He'd once briefly reflected that when he got back home he'd go look up some books on the Columbian Indian; there surely must be a treatise on these most unique people.

She said, 'You are wondering: Why did I agree to marry her tonight?'

He came back to reality very slowly, shook his head and turned. She was abundantly curvaceous with exquisite features. 'I'd be an utter fool if I didn't pinch myself to make certain of this great good fortune, Eloise. Of all the outlandish places to find you.'

'Leonard, would you rather we waited. Perhaps if we went home for a few months and you saw me in an environment which is more natural to both. . .'

'It couldn't possibly make any difference,' he said, and swept her into his arms. She weakly protested; they would most certainly be observed like this. He didn't think so, but then as he said he couldn't conceivably have cared less.

He kissed her, let her step back but clung to both her hands, and waited for whatever she might say. There really wasn't much *to* say—or else there was *too* much for any great part of it to be said in the short space of time before they'd have to return to the office to the wretched anguish of Mayor Sanchez, of Father Eusebio Lopez, and the witless young girl who'd caused it all.

'Did I tell you,' he said, knowing perfectly well he hadn't told her, 'that I inherited a stone cottage on a small acreage in the country at home, and that I go up there every week-end I can possibly get out of London, and vegetate?'

She smiled. 'You hadn't told me, but then I didn't tell you I have a deplorable affliction also: I simply adore cottages in the country. If I had my way I'd never go into a large city.' She gestured. 'I could have got Rio or Brasilia, Bogotá or Cuzco and here I am in a wretched mud village called Puna.'

Remembering something Narcisso Pinzon had told him the day he'd first arrived, he now said, 'The village you found picturesque, the people dirty and ignorant.'

She nodded. 'Does it show that much?'

'Well, not so much the past week or so, Eloise, but before I came it showed.'

She studied his face. 'I see. Someone told you. In other words, the natives weren't quite taken with me.'

'No.' If he expected anger, denunciation, recrimination, he was disappointed. She looked out where the shadows were lengthening.

'I can't actually say that I blame them, Leonard. They were so—different. So impassive and silent and phlegmatic, like cattle. Instead of the babble of an English hospital here you'll have twenty or thirty of them in the room with you and not a sound—not a cough; not even a sniffle. It makes you—well—a little fearful of them.'

'Do you feel that way now?'

She shook her head. 'Not since you came. I don't mean only because of you—I mean—well—as an example, I'd never really spoken to George Ritter Avila. I'd seen him a hundred times but we'd never spoken. And there was Mayor Sanchez—until you came he was very polite, removed his hat when we met, but said practically nothing. And Pinzon... I could name two dozen who treated me like that. Then you made them all come to life, Leonard. You made them laugh and swear and cry and turn out to be human beings no different from other human beings.'

He said dryly, 'Don't blame me, love, blame Elfego Sanchez's daughter. She was the crisis as well as the catalyst.'

'Which reminds me,' she said, turning towards the building, but he brushed it aside, knowing what she meant.

'Let them wait a bit. Elfego will be blubbering, his daughter will be sunk into a thralldom of wretched shame, Father Lopez, will be calling upon the saints, Candidly, Eloise, the kind of demonstrations these people are capable of leaves me a little detached.'

'You're cold.'

He looked at her. 'Maybe. Wouldn't that be a terrible thing to discover after we're married—that you'd got a bad bargain.'

'I was joking,' she said. 'If I'd ever thought you were cold—well—we wouldn't be out here like this right now. We most certainly wouldn't be getting married.'

They stood breathing the winey Columbian air, hearing the soft, ageless sounds of the town around them, watching their world subtly change towards mid-afternoon. After some reflection he said he thought she should go to the Sanchez home afterwards, with Elfego, and stay with Elfego's wife until she'd got over her relieved hysteria, her howling self-reproach, or whichever mood overcame her when she learned her daughter was safe and sound, and reasonably well.

She wasn't enthusiastic but she agreed.

He reached, drew her face close, kissed her, turned, and holding her hand, would have gone into the building but someone cleared his throat with considerable effort. They both looked round, surprised.

Narcisso Pinzon stepped forth from the edge of the dispensary. He smiled somewhat apologetically then said something that made them both laugh.

'I tell you something, *amigos*, it was a long wait. I have never believed a man had the right to interrupt something like—well—when friends embrace, you see. But I keep looking at my wristwatch.' Narcisso dolefully shook his head over the considerable waste of time.

Eloise said, 'Were you round that corner all the time?'

Narcisso shrugged. 'Well, *Señorita*, you said you thought it was maybe a good idea for you both to wait and see how each other looked back home. And *he* said . . .' The Indian face broke into a slow, sly smile. 'I guess I was around there a long time.'

They laughed. Narcisso broadly smiled but didn't make a sound. Later, he said to Leonard, 'The tears and things you don't like in Columbians, Doctor, are not from the Indian blood. That is from the Spanish. The Indian feels as you feel. Do something; right or wrong as you must but afterwards take what comes, don't be like old women.' Pinzon's obsidian eyes lingered on Leonard, whom he was obviously fond of. 'But I was looking for you to tell you of something.'

'All right, Narcisso, what is it?'

'I don't like to tell you, Doctor.' Narcisso was impassively standing there. Leonard had a flutter in in his stomach. For something to be bad to one of these descendants of the bloody Mayans, it would have to be very bad.

'Doctor, that lieutenant of the soldiers said *Señor* Lleras was not carrying out his orders.'

'He arrested Lleras?'

'No. He shot Jorge Avila.'

Leonard's breath caught in his throat. He and

Eloise stood rooted while Narcisso impassively stood before them, black eyes totally unreadable.

Eloise whispered: 'Good Lord!'

Leonard, gazing at Pinzon, divined there was more. He urged the Indian to tell them the whole story. Pinzon obliged.

'He went to arrest Jorge Avila, and of course as you must know by now, *Don* Jorge is not a man to be played with by young lieutenants. His men surrounded the soldiers. Lieutenant Elizondo drew his pistol and said he would shoot *Señor* Avila if the gauchos did not disband. They did not obey.' Narcisso's heavy shoulders rose and fell. 'Lieutenant Elizondo shot Jorge Avila.'

Leonard could envisage the rest of it. He'd seen the blue-black, oily automatic arms of Elizondo's detachment. 'Massacre,' he murmured.

'Oh no, Doctor,' exclaimed Narcisso. 'From the ground *Señor* Avila ordered his men to go away and not to raise so much as one machete against the soldiers. He also said the first gaucho who fired a weapon, he would personally have his liver for supper.'

'You mean Avila isn't dead?'

'No, Doctor, that's why I was looking for you. They are bringing him to the dispensary.'

Leonard and Eloise exchanged a glance. Narcisso wasn't quite finished. He added one more piece of information as the three of them turned to enter the dispensary.

'His gauchos are bringing him. I tell you something, Doctor; *Señor* Avila's men are not common campesinos. It is a known fact all of them have at one time or another been *bandoleros*. When they come to Puna—

maybe fifty of them—and they drink a little while, waiting for you to fix their *jefe*, and see those soldiers around town...' Narcisso didn't finish. He didn't have to.

Leonard felt the tension tightening his stomach again. He told Narcisso to stand out front and as soon as Jorge Avila arrived, to come let Leonard know. He then took Eloise and briskly went to his office where, to his surprise, he found only one of Eloise's dark little native nurses. The two older men were gone. He asked where the mayor and priest were. They had departed a short while earlier, he was informed, to go sit up with *Señora* Sanchez.

Leonard told Eloise to take the native nurse and go prepare with her for surgery. When he was alone he swore heartily. He'd had a bad feeling about Lieutenant Elizondo from their first meeting.

He speculated on that terrible massacre at the school so many years earlier, wondering if the officer in command of the machine-gunners hadn't been such a person as Honorio Elizondo.

Of course, when he had a few free minutes, he'd call to Bogotá and lodge a formal protest. But he would also make it a particular point to learn all he could of the shooting. Not that he doubted Narcisso Pinzon, but because there had to be more details.

Outside, the day was edging along towards pre-evening. The sun still rode across the high-arching skies but there were thin shadows lying in the plaza, people were finishing their daily work, food was cooking, and very little more that was dramatic could still occur in broad daylight.

He heard someone's high, distant cry, thought it

A Doctor in Exile

might be one of Jorge Avila's gauchos approaching, turned and walked out of his office to stand in the big empty reception room waiting. Narcisso poked his head in from the roadway. 'They are coming,' he said.

Chapter Seventeen

The sight was not very reassuring. Leonard went out into the shadowy plaza to supervise the unloading of George Ritter Avila but the gauchos did not allow Leonard nor anyone else around. They closed ranks and presented wide backs.

Across the road two armed soldiers in front of the jailhouse stood uneasily. Up the road on the far side of the INCORA building not far from the hotel, where the barracks were, other soldiers stood, also armed and —or so it appeared to Leonard—in greater numbers out there than was customary.

He'd ignored the soldiers until he saw them standing around up there armed and watchful, then his nerves tingled; he didn't only have the shooting of the most influential landowner to worry about, or the presence of that landowner's tough, willing workmen, he also had an unpredictable lieutenant and a detachment of soldiers as well.

He helped Narcisso hold the doors as Avila was carried inside. Not until they were into the reception room did the gauchos offer to let Leonard look. He told them to take their *patrón* into an examination room and led the way. He motioned for Narcisso to come along. As the gauchos were crowding in with Avila, Eloise and her native nurse appeared, curtly ordering more than two-thirds of the gauchos away.

Leonard asked Narcisso if it had also looked to him as though someone had ordered those soldiers to gather out front of the barracks, armed. Narcisso said it had appeared that way to him and of course it would also appear that way to the gauchos.

'Can you locate the lieutenant?' asked Leonard.

Narcisso foresaw no vast difficulty in that accomplishment. He would go at once and see about it.

'Tell him Dr Bordon would like to see him at the dispensary. Tell him it is vitality important. And Narcisso—try and come up with something that might prevent a fight here tonight.'

Narcisso shrugged. He would of course get the officer and he would stress how important that it would be for Elizondo to talk to Dr Bordon, but as for thinking of some way to avoid bloodshed, he obviously considered the possibility extremely remote, and his expression told Leonard that Narcisso was not convinced Avila's men weren't entitled to kill a few soldiers.

Eloise came briskly to summon Leonard. As he turned to go several of the Avila gauchos came forward. One spoke church-school English. He wished to know that *Dón* Jorge would recover satisfactorily. Leonard recognized one of the Indians as the thickly made bandy-legged man he and Ed Lleras had met at the *estancia*.

All he could tell the men was that he would do what he could. They had to be satisfied with that too, because he walked away with Eloise Cutler.

She had made a cursory examination also. The bullet, having been fired at close quarters should ordinarily have done irreparable damage, but there were two saving factors. One, the bullet was steel-jacketed and had not mushroomed upon impact as a lead slug would have done, and two, the pistol was one of those ultra-modern weapons rated by magnum fire-power; it sent its projective so incredibly swiftly that when such a bullet struck that close it went completely through whatever it struck almost with the same searing affect as a laser light. There wasn't even very much shock.

But when Leonard stepped to the stripped huge body covered from the waist down by a light sheet, he saw that the bullet had angled upwards, penetrating George Ritter Avila's abdomen and lung. It had emerged to the right of Avila's right shoulderblade without nicking the bone.

Altogether, the wound was serious but not necessarily fatal. Avila's tawny eyes followed Leonard's every move but he said nothing. When Eloise leaned to say something, across from Leonard, the big man smiled up at her. Leonard saw that.

There was little that could be done for the wound. As soon as it could be determined Avila was not seriously bleeding internally, he would then need rest and quiet above everything else for the long period of recuperation. Movement could conceivably start a haemorrhage. Of course he would have to be injected with anti-bacterins and perhaps, when restlessness took over, also with relaxants and tranquillizers.

Leonard explained all this. Avila, with a thin line of blood on his lips, whispered that he was in favour of the long rest, that he felt very tired now.

Leonard asked about the shooting. Avila said it was an accident. Leonard told him what he knew. The gold-flecked eyes turned sardonic.

'You have spies,' he whispered. 'All right; that is how it happened. The lieutenant is a fool, but I was

143

also to blame. I had no idea he was so nervous. I argued.'

Eloise frowned across at Leonard. She patently didn't think Avila should be talking. Leonard ignored the frown and said, 'What was Elizondo trying to do?'

'Arrest me. He said I was interfering with the Land Reform.'

'Was Ed Lleras with him?'

'No.'

Finally Eloise spoke. 'Doctor...' She said it in quiet but firm protest and Leonard nodded, telling her to take over. He then went out front, saw the gauchos hunkering around dark and silent, some smoking, some dozing, and sent one of them for Ed Lleras at either the INCORA office or the hotel, then he went into the office to wait.

Oddly enough, Lleras arrived first. In fact Lieutenant Elizondo didn't arrive until nearly a half hour after Lleras although Narcisso certainly had found him much earlier.

Leonard asked Lleras what he knew of the incident at Avila's *estancia*. Ed was pale and shaken. He knew only what everyone else in town had heard: That Lieutenant Elizondo had shot Jorge Ritter Avila. But he had more interest in the matter than most. As he told Leonard, this was precisely what he'd wanted so very much to avoid.

'Now look out there; armed soldiers jumpy as cats and those confounded cowboys of Avila's sitting round like a herd of jaguars waiting for the opportune moment so they can attack the soldiers. Elizondo will of course be blamed in Bogotá, Doctor, but do you know what they will do to me? Remove me. Send someone else here to administer the land reform program. I will be classified incapable of performing jobs requiring tact and initiative. I will have failed.'

'That's all in the future,' said Leonard, a trifle impatient. 'What I'd like to know is by what authority Elizondo drove out to the *estancia*. Does he have the right to do that without orders from you or someone else?'

'He has. He went to great pains to explain to me on the drive here that his orders were to make certain dissident factions or bandits—*bandoleros*—were not allowed to interfere; that he was to suppress disorders any way he saw fit.'

Leonard dropped down behind his table. 'What kind of military system puts a man like Elizondo, who is obviously emotionally immature and unstable in charge of pacifying a countryside to begin with, and gives him a free hand as to how to do it?'

Ed Lleras looked unhappy. 'Doctor,' he said softly, pensively, 'since being back in my native land I've made an unpleasant discovery. I'm not a Columbian. As a child I was, but the kind of education my parents gave me is a curse. I don't belong with these people. They irritate me with their cruelty, they annoy me with their childishness, but above all, they make me feel alien with their hidebound unwillingness to depart from the practices their own tyrants used, and which they themselves rebelled against.

'I came back here to help my native land move up into the modern world. And here I am, chided for being too slow with the land reform, saddled with a glory-hunter soldier, stopped in my tracks by Avila, and now sitting on a powder keg waiting for one Indian cowboy or one noisy soldier to start the slaughter. I know what's wrong. I know what should be done. And I can't do a damned thing about any of it.'

Someone rapped on the office door. Leonard called for them to enter. It was Lieutenant Honorio Elizondo with a sergeant. Elizondo coldly gazed at Lleras, at Leonard, told his sergeant to stand vigil outside the door, and closed the panel.

Leonard did not arise but he pointed to a vacant chair. Lieutenant Elizondo ignored the chair and flushed slightly at Leonard's deliberate rudeness. 'I have my duties,' he said to Leonard, 'so please be brief, Doctor.'

Ed Lleras looked up sharply on the verge of commenting. Leonard spoke first. 'Lieutenant, will you explain to me exactly why you shot Jorge Avila this afternoon?'

Elizondo's cold face turned hostile. 'I have just completed a written report to my superiors, Doctor. In time, if you make the request, they might send you a copy.'

Leonard unwound up out of his chair angry and quick. 'Was he armed, Lieutenant; was he threatening you; when we first met you made some remarks about knowing what your duty was. I may be somewhat rusty as to what constitutes a soldier's duty, Lieutenant, but I knew very well what *humane* obligations are, and attempted murder, seeking to incite civil insurrection, are not included.'

Elizondo's black eyes brightened with cold wrath. 'Doctor, you are only a guest of my country. You don't understand our politics nor our systems. In fact, you don't even speak our language very well.'

'What in the hell,' demanded Ed Lleras, springing out of his chair, 'has any of that got to with behaving

146

like an armed madman at the Avila *estancia*, Lieutenant?'

Elizondo turned in a flash. He'd been restrained in his dealings with Leonard, but Lleras was a countryman. His words struck hard. 'You, *Señor*,' he said angrily, 'don't belong. You aren't even a Columbian. But let me tell you something: I *am* the authority here. I can have *you* shot!'

Leonard moved to head off a physical encounter. As he stepped between the younger men he said, 'Lieutenant, if there is a battle in Magdalena Valley over what you've done, it will be your fault and I'll damned well see that Bogotá knows that one fact!'

Elizondo, hooking thumbs in his garrison belt, looked scornful. 'For two hundred years you foreigners have made trouble for us, Doctor. Well, not any more. We are just as worldy wise, just as educated as you are. No one in Bogotá will take the word of a foreigner against the word of a Columbian army officer.'

Lleras made a little choking sound and stepped back to his chair, grey and limp. Leonard waited, unwilling to trust himself to speak for a moment. When control returned he tried another tack.

'Lieutenant, do us all a favour. Confine your soldiers to barracks. Keep them off the streets until Mr Lleras and I can get rid of *Señor* Avila's men. Help us to this extent and the three of us can perhaps prevent a battle.'

'I do not fear a battle, Doctor.'

'Then you are a bigger fool than I thought, Lieutenant. You're not the only one in this room who has been in a war. It's criminal to provoke hostilities when there is no real need.'

147

Elizondo dropped his arms, clenched both fists and said huskily. 'Did you call me a fool, Doctor?'

Leonard paused. It wasn't the imminence of physical violence that turned him cold and thoughtful. It was the sickening knowledge that he might as well be talking to a stone wall. Honorio Elizondo was a demagogue; a junior officer itching to show his mettle against enemies.

'Doctor, I am awaiting your answer!'

Leonard nodded. 'I called you a fool, Lieutenant. If I could think of a more appropriate name I'd call you that too.'

Elizondo snarled and lunged. It was a typical barracks-brawl type manoeuvre and perhaps against men like himself Elizondo might have prevailed, but Leonard Bordon, one-time middleweight boxing champion, inter-collegiate as well as regimental, was far from being a novice. He stepped half away then stepped back again. As Elizondo's straining body hurtled past, Leonard dropped the lieutenant with a savage strike behind and below the left ear.

Elizondo didn't even turn, didn't even try to halt his momentum. He struck the table, knocked it over and fell into a limp heap behind it.

Ed Lleras was petrified. It had all happened very fast. Leonard was flexing his right hand when Lleras arose, went over and bent to look.

'He's out cold,' he said, in quiet awe. 'How did you do it?'

Leonard ignored the question to say, 'If our lieutenant isn't any better in battle than he is in a brawl, he'll get himself killed before long. Lend a hand, Ed, we'll disarm him, tie his hands, then I'll call Bogotá. There's going to be a fuss over this.'

Lleras was troubled. 'Doctor, with that damned road closed, Elizondo and his soldiers are the major force here. If you make him a prisoner, the soldiers will riot. We'll have exactly the bloodshed we don't want.'

Leonard disarmed the unconscious officer and got some tape to bind his arms with. He didn't ask Lleras to assist again. Afterwards, he went to the table, set it upright, sat down and put in his call to Bogotá. He was breathing hard.

Chapter Eighteen

It was dark out but neither Ed Lleras nor Leonard were even remotely concerned with that. Lleras stood over Lieutenant Elizondo, seemingly stricken with doubts and indecision. Leonard was on the telephone to Bogotá. He had a long wait while the chairman of the United Nations Columbian Committee, a Columbian himself, was located and brought to the telephone. He pleasantly informed Dr Bordon he'd been taken away from his dinner.

Leonard didn't bother apologizing. He told the official in short, blunt sentences, precisely what the situation was in Magdalena Valley. Afterwards there was a long silence, then the smooth, bland voice from Bogotá changed; it became cold and sharp. First, Leonard was remonstrated for striking a Columbian army officer, then he was told the matter would have to be laid before the Columbian Republic's Army Chief of Staff. Finally, he was informed that despite the lateness, an inspection team of top government officials would be dispatched to Puna at once.

When Leonard explained about the road, the Columbian said the team would be flown in. The last thing he said was for Leonard to do whatever he must to keep the peace, but that everything would now be on Leonard's shoulders.

As he hung up, Leonard turned towards Ed Lleras.

'We're going to have an official visit by air,' he informed the younger man. 'And I shocked the hell out of the U.N. representative.'

Ed looked ruefully at Elizondo. 'You shocked hell out of him too. He's coming round. Now what do we do?'

'You had better leave so he'll only blame me.'

'I'll stay, Doctor.' Lleras looked glum but dogged. 'I can't be in any more hot water than I'm already in anyway.'

Leonard went over to gaze at the army officer. Elizondo's focusing eyes settled upon Leonard as though he were trying to recall something. Eventually they cleared and a look of incredulity lingered briefly, then Elizondo spat out a Spanish curse. 'I'll have you shot, Doctor!'

Leonard was sanguine about that. 'First you'll have to leave here to give the order, Lieutenant.'

'You can't hold me, Doctor.'

'I'm doing it, Lieutenant.'

Elizondo looked at Lleras. 'If he is a madman, *Señor*, you had better not be influenced. He can't hold me indefinitely and when I am released I'll see to it that you stand to the wall beside him.'

Lleras didn't even answer. He went to the window and looked out. There was a sliver of moon amid a galaxy of blue-white stars.

The officer swore again. Leonard leaned down. 'The next time you refer to either of us in an uncomplimentary manner, I'm going to release you—then beat you within an inch of your life.'

Elizondo's wrath didn't diminish but his discretion came to the fore. He still didn't know how Leonard had knocked him senseless, but he knew for a fact it had

151

happened. He studied Leonard for a moment before speaking again, his voice slightly less antagonistic.

'Doctor, if you think detaining me is going to prevent trouble, you are wrong. I can only prevent trouble if I am set free.'

Leonard smiled and walked off. In fact he left the room for a brief time and returned, still smiling. Neither Lleras nor the lieutenant had any idea what he had done until he told them.

'All I did, Lieutenant, was relay your orders to the sergeant.'

'What orders?'

'The orders you asked me to carry out to him. The orders directing that he take the soldiers—including the jailhouse guards—up to the barracks and confine all men to the barracks until further notice.'

The lieutenant's face swelled with fury. He mightily strained at the bonds holding both arms behind him. He looked as though he would curse, too, but Ed Lleras walked over, raised him off the floor and dumped him upon a chair which appeared to at least change Elizondo's immediate centre of concentration.

He watched Leonard cross to the desk, drop into a chair beyond it, then he made a fierce threat. 'Doctor, you have broken any number of Columbian laws. I warned you I'd have you shot. Now I *promise* you that!'

Eloise came knocking. So she wouldn't see the hostage Leonard crossed swiftly to open the door himself. She said George Ritter Avila wished to see him. He tried suggesting in the morning, that it was very late, but Eloise shook her head.

'When *Señor* Avila calls, no one keeps him waiting until morning.'

From the corner of his eye Leonard saw the

lieutenant open his mouth—and Ed Lleras's hand suddenly slap down hard over the opening. Without another word Leonard stepped through, closed the door and walked towards the ward with Eloise.

She told him something odd had happened. There wasn't a solitary armed soldier on the streets nor in the plaza, not even across the road at the jailhouse. He told her she had no idea just how really odd that was.

Avila looked pale, which seemed odd. Every other time Leonard had seen the big man he'd been ruddily menacing and disgustingly healthy. He looked long at Leonard then said huskily because all round them in the ward patients were sleeping,' Doctor; send Miss Cutler away. What I have to say is private.'

Leonard gave no such order. 'Mr Avila, whatever you have to say, Miss Cutler can hear.'

Avila frowned. He flicked a look at Eloise and licked his lips. 'Doctor, the boy—his mother raised him. I only knew two years ago he was mine. I have to tell you what she did for her revenge against me. She taught him to despise landowners. I tried to give him work. He refused. I offered him a few sections of land. He said he wouldn't spit on land I'd once owned.' Avila sighed. 'Well, I'll give you back the money you gave him because you settled something for the boy and for me. I didn't know what to do with him. You solved it.'

He solved it when he played games with Sanchez's daughter.'

'All right, have it your way. Doctor . . .?'

'Yes.'

'About that land. Tell Lleras he can have it. I don't want his money. Tell him to bring me the papers. I'll sign them. The government will pay me five times what those useless plains are worth anyway.'

Leonard smiled and reached to gingerly clasp Avila's left hand in a grip, then release it. 'All Ed Lleras ever needed, Mr Avila, was one decent break. He's the kind of young man Columbia needs.' As he straightened up Leonard said, 'About the other landowners. . .?'

'I'll have them sign also. It will take a little time to mail out the forms for their signatures, and to receive them back again. But I'll guarantee it.'

'I'll send him to you, Mr Avila. Tell him this yourself. And by the way; that lieutenant who shot you—he is tied up in my office. A helicopter of high government officials is flying in tonight to investigate.'

'*Tied*, Doctor. . .?'

Leonard felt Eloise staring and said, 'Well, a man has a right to defend himself, even in Columbia, hasn't he? The lieutenant lunged at me. I knocked him out, took away his pistol and used medical adhesive to bind his wrists. It was nothing, really, although the lieutenant has promised to shoot me the minute he is released.'

Avila's eyes lit up with a tough, sardonic smile. 'Doctor,' he said. 'Find Alfredo. Have him come to me here at once.'

'What for?'

'Well Doctor, you've quieted the military. The least I can do is quiet the gauchos.'

Leonard and Eloise were leaving the dimly lighted ward before she said, 'Leonard! You didn't strike that army officer.'

'I was a little reluctant, Eloise. A *little* reluctant, I said. The confounded idiot has been itching to start serious trouble ever since he came into the valley. I had to stop him somehow, and when he jumped at me, I stopped him.'

'And this team of high ranking government officials —what will they say, you striking, disarming and holding a Columbian army officer captive?'

She looked so deadly serious he couldn't keep from smiling as he answered. 'They can't shoot me. It would cause a scandal. Besides, with U.N. officials and observers all over the place seeing how the land redistribution works, I have a sneaky feeling they'll want the entire affair hushed up.'

She wasn't convinced, and also, she was frightened. She walked with him back to the doorway of his office, when he saw the gauchos talking with Narcisso. He called. Narcisso came at once. He told him what Avila had said, adding a suggestion of his own exactly as he'd done with the sergeant, only with Narcisso he didn't stretch the truth.

'*Dón* Jorge wants to see Alfredo, Narcisso, but I can tell you what *Dón* Jorge will tell him. All the Avila men are to return to the *estancia* and remain there—out of Puna—until *Dón* Jorge sends them different orders. All of them. There are to be no exceptions.'

Narcisso looked enormously relieved. 'Doctor, I have just been arguing with them. They say now that the soldiers are all in their barracks it would be an excellent time to set the building afire, then secrete themselves on rooftops across the plaza where they could shoot down the ones who ran out—with flames at their backs.'

Leonard felt Eloise stiffen at the calculating cruelty of this elemental plan. He shook his head. '*Dón* Jorge said he would have the liver and heart of the gaucho who disobeyed his order to return to the *estancia*.'

155

Narcisso was convinced as well as pleased, and he did precisely what Leonard had thought; he didn't go seeking his brother at all, he went directly over where the gauchos were impassively sitting, and began speaking in machine-gun Spanish.

Leonard took Eloise into the office. Ed Lleras sprang up when the door opened. When he saw who it was he relaxed. He'd been giving Elizondo a drink of water.

The lieutenant and Eloise exchanged a look. She asked if Elizondo were hurt. He looked away without answering so Ed told her only Elizondo's prickly pride had been injured.

She looked disturbed for the first time since Leonard had known her. Ordinarily she was unflappable. Of course this was something quite foreign to her daily routine. Seriously so, in fact.

He took her across to the window dropped his voice and said, 'There is something I haven't overlooked nor forgot, but I still have to apologise for it. We were to be married tonight.'

She looked at him with a little queer expression then said, 'Leonard, if they don't dare shoot you, they still have legal jurisdiction: What good is a wife to a man languishing in a Columbian jail?'

'Her memory could be an infinite solace.'

'You're being facetious at a very poor time!'

'Perhaps, love, but you are seeing peril where it might be better and wait to see what develops. By the way, how is the Sanchez girl?'

His calm had its effect. She said Elena was sleeping very comfortably. 'I put Felicidad to watching over her. If it seems a strange pair, it really isn't. Felicidad is wise far beyond her seventeen years. She can give

156

Elena Sanchez a lot of bitter but very candid and practical advice when Elena wakes up.'

He agreed, then turned to see both Ed Lleras and Honorio Elizondo watching them. 'Ed, why don't you take those government forms for the land in to Mr Avila,' he said quietly. 'He has agreed to sign them and relinquish the land to the government.'

Lleras stood a moment with his mouth open, then he jumped up without a word and went flinging out of the office. Only Elizondo's bitter, hating face was left and there was no way to deal with that. He sent Eloise for black coffee for the lieutenant and himself, then sat at the table feeling much better, for some reason, than he'd felt in days.

'Lieutenant, I appreciate your intense patriotism, but I seriously question your motives. If you had in mind making yourself some kind of hero by suppressing Avila, believe me it wouldn't have worked out that way. You are brave, of course, but you just aren't very intelligent. When the government officials arrive. . . .'

'I demand the right to speak to them at once!' exclaimed Elizondo.

Leonard nodded coolly. 'You shall have that privilege. But let me suggest one word of advice: The pistol went off accidentally.'

'That is a lie!'

Leonard smiled thinly. 'You know it, Avila and I know it, but the government officials won't and Avila can be induced to help salvage your reputation I'm sure. Think it over, Lieutenant.'

Elizondo made a strangling sound of fury deep in his throat but Leonard was reaching for that unfinished report and ignored both the officer and the sound.

Chapter Nineteen

They got a little asleep, all but Lieutenant Elizondo and even he may have cat-napped in his chair, but when dawn came the dispensary routine awakened them all.

Father Lopez came while the ward patients were being fed. He shared a cup of coffee with Eloise and Leonard in the large reception room which, since it was quite early, hadn't yet begun to fill up with its shuffling daily load of ill and uncomfortable natives.

Eusebio Lopez related the experiences he'd had since the evening before. The mayor's wife had cried a little for the lost virtue of her daughter, but only just enough to be proper on that issue, then she'd been so relieved that her Elena was alive and unhurt she'd insisted on getting out of bed, weak as she was. Only her husband's dogged insistence prevented her from dressing and going straightaway to the dispensary. Also, said Father Lopez, some neighbours arrived to whisper of the wanton shooting of *Dón* Jorge Avila, and to prudently suggest that no one leave the Sanchez home because there were tense, armed soldiers in the plaza as well as a great many hostile gauchos.

He had prayed with the Sanchezes, and when he was sure he'd fall asleep on his feet, the mayor's wife made them black coffee and fried chorizo, both of which were hot enough to dispel any notions of sleep.

158

Father Lopez then asked about the shooting. Leonard told him while Eloise went off at the call of one of nurses to see to some particular patient. As soon as she was gone Leonard asked if Father Lopez would marry them. Neither man mentioned that both Leonard and Eloise were not Catholics. Father Lopez, in fact, acted as though it were a foregone conclusion that they *were* of his church, which may—or may not—have been a slight oversight.

He agreed at once, acting delighted at the prospect. He also said, when Leonard told him they were all waiting the arrival of government officials, that whatever action Leonard had taken to prevent a battle last night, he was four-square behind him.

Leonard smiled, led Eusebio Lopez over to the office, opened the door and pointed at Lieutenant Elizondo.

Father Lopez nearly dropped his coffee cup. Leonard closed the door and explained. Father Lopez remained loyal but very clearly this was something altogether different from preventing battles, repairing damaged families, even saving the life of Jorge Avila.

'The law is very specific,' he told Leonard. 'Anyone interfering with the army in the performance of its duties is classified a pirate. They are to be executed within fifteen minutes of apprehension. Doctor, I think you'd better release the lieutenant, give him back his gun and make peace with him.'

'Not much chance, Father,' explained Leonard. 'The moment I hand him back his gun he will shoot me. He has promised to do that.'

Father Lopez recovered most of his equanimity with second cup of black coffee. 'Well,' he muttered, 'then because all of this is tied together, I will go mention

159

to Mayor Sanchez and some others that you have single-handedly prevented a massacre here, and undoubtedly they will support you against the lieutenant. But Doctor—that marriage may have to be postponed.'

Father Lopez was grimly dogged when he departed. Even when he'd been hiding Elena Sanchez in his church he hadn't looked as bleak as he did now.

Narcisso came in from the plaza accompanied by his brother, Alfredo. They had just returned from the Avila *estancia*, stated Narcisso, and the last of the gauchos was up there. 'Alfredo came back with me but only to see *Don* Jorge then he will go back again.'

Leonard sent them on into the ward, but as they departed he considered Alfredo unfavourably. Of all the gauchos, Alfredo was perhaps the least trustworthy. He wished Narcisso had not brought him back.

Ed Lleras poked his head in to say there was a helicopter approaching from above the northeastern mountains. Fr Lopez, Ed also reported, was running through town like the devil after a crippled saint.

Leonard finished his coffee, told Ed he'd join him outside after a bit, and went in search of Eloise. As it happened she was coming in search of him and they met in the corridor beyond the ward.

'The officials are arriving,' he stated. 'I'll go meet them.'

'Leonard. . .?'

At the look of anxiety in her eyes, he stretched forth a hand to lightly pat her cheek. 'It can't be all that bad, love. You keep everyone here happy, or at least comfortable, and I'll come to you as quickly as I can.'

She kissed him, turned swiftly and hastened back into the ward. He didn't see her face but then, he hadn't had to see it. He knew when a woman was on the verge of losing control. He also approved of her return to duty. The best of all therapies was work.

Narcisso was nowhere around when Leonard joined young Ed Lleras outside. There was considerable interest throughout Puna; not many natives had seen wingless helicopters before although they'd all seen winged aircraft, and none of them had ever seen a helicopter up close. With children whooping and running towards the southerly end of the village where an untended airfield lay, the adults trudged along also.

Then, Leonard saw Narcisso. He was driving his old automobile. Ed Lleras smiled. Speaking of the officials he said, 'They may be a little shaken by Pinzon's car and the multitude of urchins and Indians, but they'll never be able to say Puna didn't turn out to properly welcome them.'

Leonard said nothing. Perhaps the officials might be favourably impressed, perhaps not, but in any event neither he nor Ed Lleras had much cause for elation. He was perfectly satisfied with his own actions, but as had been somewhat forcefully pointed out by Fr Lopez, this was not his native land; things were viewed—and done—differently, in Columbia.

Up the road Honorio Elizondo's sergeant strolled forth from the barracks smoking a cigarette. He studied the empty plaza, saw Ed and Leonard, and came strolling towards them. He was a thick, very dark, placid-faced mestizo with coarse but amiable features. He smiled easily when he came abreast and said in soft Spanish, 'What is all the celebration about, gentlemen?'

Ed told him in Spanish that some government officials were arriving south of town. The sergeant accepted this with only one comment, 'Perhaps that

161

is where the lieutenant is. We have been wondering. He didn't return last night.'

Leonard avoided Ed's glance and instead watched the sergeant's cigarette rise in a spinning arc and drop far out into the roadway dust where it had been propelled.

Ed then asked if the sergeant had seen the shooting yesterday. The soldier nodded, losing most of his little amiable smile. 'I was there,' he said. 'It was a very bad moment, *Señores*. Of course we had the firepower, but if *Señor* Avila hadn't prevented it, I think all the firepower in the world wouldn't have prevented something very bad. There were many more gauchos than soldiers.'

Leonard turned to consider the burly, dark soldier. 'It was not a very wise thing, your officer did,' he said in Spanish.

The sergeant's black eyes shifted to Leonard and lingered. 'Perhaps not, but I am only a common soldier.' The dark eyes reproached Leonard but the man said no more. Obviously, he resented the criticism from an outsider.

Leonard understood the sergeant's attitude. It was reasonable under the circumstances, in a place such as Magdalena Valley. He said, 'I don't mean to criticise, Sergeant. I only want to prevent serious trouble.'

The sergeant's smile returned. 'Of course, *Señor*. My personal feelings are that there really is no need. Sugar catches more flies than vinegar, no?'

Leonard smiled back.

Narcisso's old car was grandly chuffing up towards the plaza creating a veil of thin ochre-coloured dust. Far back came the people, led as before by swift-footed urchins. Ed Lleras let his breath out and fidgeted.

Narcisso was driving slowly. Leonard made a shrewd guess about that. Narcisso had the government officials all to himself for this short ride; he would be giving them the basic facts of all that had occurred over the past twenty-four hours. It was a good thing Narcisso was on Leonard's side.

The old car halted our front of the dispensary and the first man out, after Narcisso, was Elfego Sanchez. The next two men were crisp, amooth-faced, authoritative individuals dressed in army fatigue uniforms without insignias of rank. Nonetheless, the sergeant sprang to attention and saluted.

Mayor Sanchez made the introductions. Leonard and Ed Lleras shook hands with General Francisco Miranda and Colonel Olmega Ortez. Both officers peered closely at Leonard, did not smile when they shook hands, and finally returned the sergeant's salute as they moved past to enter the dispensary. By that time the crowd was coming up; voices made a low continuous hum on all sides. Narcisso, standing near his old car, caught Leonard's eye and gravely winked. He had done all he could, from here on it would have to be up to others.

Inside the dispensary Eloise and one of her little nurses had a surprise: Fresh coffee. The high-ranking officers smiled for the first time. They evidently needed that coffee. Eloise offered to have breakfast sent but the general declined, turning to gaze over where people were crowding inside. He shot Leonard an inquiring look. In faultless English he said, 'They can't all be ill, can they?'

Leonard asked Ed Lleras to suggest that the people wait outside unless of course they were sick. In the forefront stood old Raymond Reyes from whose eyes

Leonard had removed the cataracts. Alfredo was also there along with a dozen other men Leonard had patched up or whom Eloise had cared for. They backed out of the building but reluctantly and the general, sipping coffee, made a shrewd guess.

'Your former patients, Doctor? You have made friends here.' He put aside the cup and turned to make another impassive study of Leonard. 'Where is the young lieutenant?'

Leonard pointed towards his office door.

General Miranda looked blandly at the door and looked back. 'He is unable to come out?'

'His arms are taped behind his back, General.'

Miranda showed no surprise at the comment but he kept staring at Leonard as though he might have something to say about that. In the end, though, he walked over, flung open the door and stood gazing in. The others joined him. It was very quiet except for that low drone of voices just beyond the roadway door.

Lieutenant Elizondo stood at attention, his face scarlet, his black eyes venomously, accusingly, upon Leonard. He stated his name and rank, then said he could not salute for obvious reasons, and taking back one big breath, launched into a fierce tirade against Dr Bordon. The general walked in and sought a chair without a word. The colonel was next. He snarled two words at Lieutenant Elizondo: 'Be quiet!'

Ed Lleras hesitated in the doorway until Leonard gave him a slight shove. They were all inside when Leonard then closed the door. Colonel Ortez remained standing. His face was less bland than General Miranda's; Ortez glared at Elizondo.

Miranda said pleasantly to Leonard, 'Did you ever ride over some of the highest mountains in America in the dark—in a helicopter, Doctor?'

'No, General.'

'It is nothing anyone in his right mind would volunteer for believe me." He motioned for Leonard and Ed Lleras to be seated and finally got round to addressing Lieutenant Elizondo. 'In due course I will see your official report, Lieutenant, so for now I only want you to answer one question for me. I want no alibis, no polemics, just one simple answer.'

Elizondo stood very erect. 'Yes, *mi general.*'

'Lieutenant, this man you shot—were you aware he was the brother-in-law of the President of the Republic?'

Leonard was stunned. So, evidently, was Honorio Elizondo. Ed Lleras stood mouth agape. Elizondo's reply was almost a whisper.

'No, *mi general.*'

Miranda thinly smiled. 'I thought not. Now then, Lieutenant, the one question you will answer for me: The gun in your hand—it discharged accidentally?'

Leonard saw sweat on Elizondo's forehead. The young officer's agonized eyes swing a little and met Leonard's gaze. Leonard gave his head the smallest of forward nods. Honorio Elizondo said, again speaking in that hoarse whisper: 'Yes sir, it discharged accidentally.'

General Miranda was still being very bland but Colonel Ortez still glared. Miranda sighed, smiled and said, 'Of course, Lieutenant, for otherwise if an officer were to shoot down the brother-in-law of *el Presidente* he would of course have to be executed on the spot, wouldn't he?'

'*Si, mi general!*'

Miranda arose, turned his back on Elizondo and

said, 'Come, Doctor, I would like to visit the wounded man. Mr Lleras and Colonel Ortez will stay with the lieutenant.'

Leonard moved to open the door and lead the way to Avila's bed in the ward.

Chapter Twenty

Jorge Avila was resting well. Eloise had taken care of
the sedation but in any event there wouldn't have been
much pain, simply the sense of weakness, of lassitude.
Leonard, as he'd led General Miranda to the bed, had
been trying to devise some way to warn Avila of the
proper answers in advance, which of course he couldn't
possibly do because Miranda understood English very
well too. What Leonard was not fully aware of yet was
that Francisco Miranda did not want to find reasons
to execute Lieutenant Elizondo.

Avila smiled slightly when Leonard introduced
General Miranda. In soft Spanish Avila said he was
delighted to make the acquaintance of so lofty an
officer.

Miranda's suave blandness was equal to that remark.
He said in flawless English, 'Mr Avila, it was my
honour to make the flight here to make certain everything possible was being done for you. After all, you
are very influential in Bogotá. It is *my* honour and
privilege I assure you.'

Avila's gold-flecked eyes turned sardonic. In English
he said, 'General, if we couldn't speak Spanish what
a pity. English just doesn't have the words for this
kind of flowery nonsense, does it?'

Miranda looked startled, then he broke into laughter
that brought every eye in the ward to Avila's bed.

Eloise looked across at Leonard. He winked.

Miranda then proceeded to put the words into Avila's mouth very slowly. 'It is the most unfortunate of all accidents,' he said, emphasizing that last word, 'that an officer of the army should have caused your injury, *Dón* Jorge. But I bring with me the deep concern of *el Presidente*, as well, naturally, as of the President's wife, not to mention the anxiety of the Minister of War, the Minister of the Interior, and. . .'

Avila snorted. 'General,' he interrupted to say, 'I'm sure my injury will be announced as a national day of mourning.' He paused, looked at Eloise, at Leonard, winked at each of them raffishly, then continued. 'But accidents will happen.' He too emphasised the word 'Accident'. 'No doubt the lieutenant was unfamiliar with that particular weapon. A German pistol, wasn't it?'

'Yet, It was a Luger. A very tricky pistol, *Señor* Avila.'

Avila and Miranda looked each other squarely in the eye. And smiled. Leonard finally understood what was being done. No one wanted Elizondo shot, nor did any of them want an official inquiry made. Miranda sighed, looked round the ward and back again. He was his usual bland self. 'Mr Avila,' he said in English, 'if there is anything at all I can do. . .'

'There is. Take the lieutenant back to Bogotá with you.'

'It shall be done of course. I'll leave Colonel Ortez in charge here. He is very favourable to the land reform. He is also a wise and clever officer. You can depend upon his fullest co-operation.'

'I don't need his co-operation,' replied Jorge Avila. 'See that he gives it to *Señor* Lleras of INCORA.'

'Precisely as you wish,' Miranda murmured, and bowed. Straightening up he shot an admiring glance at Eloise, who hadn't moved nor spoken throughout all this. 'Señor,' he said in Spanish to Jorge Avila. 'I believe that under the circumstances, I'd like to exchange places with you.'

Avila looked at Eloise. Leonard also gazed round at her. She must have understood the general's look if not his Spanish for she was reddening. Avila said resignedly, 'It would do you no good, General. She is going to wed Dr Bordon. It is a shame, but she won't have it any other way.'

Miranda smiled at Leonard. 'In that case I volunteer to stand up with you, Doctor.'

Leonard already had an answer for that. 'I was rather hoping I could prop Mr Avila up for that duty, General—then there is one other man, an Indian named Narcisso Pinzon—I'd like to also stand up with me.'

Miranda nodded. 'Well, I must go back and explain what I want Colonel Ortez to do. Please excuse me?'

Avila watched General Miranda depart wearing a tough little saturnine smile. As the officer passed from sight Avila said, 'Doctor, of course we are still enemies you understand.'

Leonard nodded unsmilingly. 'Of course. It couldn't be any other way. Did you sign the papers for Ed Lleras?'

'I signed them. Why would you want an enemy to be your best man at a wedding?'

'Oh, one can always get friends to do that for one, Mr Avila. I've always thought it would be more interesting the other way.'

Avila raised his eyes to Eloise. 'You wouldn't reconsider? I am a rich man. I have a beautiful *estancia*. I have watched you for a year, always wondering if there wasn't some way we could properly meet.'

She surprised Leonard by being quite equal to the awkward situation. 'You should have found a way last year, Mr Avila. I too have been waiting a long while.'

Avila dropped his eyes, thought a moment, then said, 'Doctor, on one condition I will be your best man, and on one condition will I give you a wedding present.'

Leonard stood silent. He knew Avila was enough of a non-conformist to make this offer in good faith, but he was also half fearful what strings might be attached.

'Doctor, I will furnish and properly staff the new hospital for one full year, paying all salaries and Magdalena Valley for that one more full year.'

It was not a small offer; to adequately staff and support the new hospital for one year would run into thousands of pounds. But there was something else; Leonard saw the moment he looked at Eloise that she too had thought of this other thing. If they stayed, they would also be able to ensure that proper personnel and procedures would be established. In short, they'd be able to make certain the new hospital would be exactly as it should be.

Avila finally said, 'Think it over, Doctor. You too, Miss Cutler.'

Leonard took Eloise by the arm and led her out of the ward. One of the nurses was coming through in search of Leonard and they met her at the door. Her eyes were big as she said there was a deputation of citizens outside the front door desiring to speak to Leonard. He thanked her, took Eloise with him, still holding her arm, and saw at once that what the nurse had called a 'deputation' was a huge crowd that filled the road way and nearly filled the entire plaza. Elfego Sanchez was their spokesman, but Raymondo Reyes and a number of other previous patients were standing right up beside the mayor when Sanchez spoke.

'Doctor, this is a document we wish to have presented to the government officials.' He pushed the thick papers into Leonard's hand. 'It is to say that if any steps are to be taken against you for whatever reason, the people of Magdalena Valley will permit no hospital to be built at Puna; that we will destroy the landing field so no airplanes can come in here, and we'll see to it that the repaired road is dynamited at once.'

Eloise leaned closer to Leonard to say, 'I think we'd better accept Avila's offer. It is beginning to appear to me that we *have* to accept it, otherwise there will be new trouble.'

Leonard nodded at Elfego Sanchez. 'I'll see that General Miranda is given this document,' he said. 'Now please—send everyone home, *Señor Sanchez*.' He switched to Spanish and raised his voice so the crowding people could hear too. 'Rest tranquil, friends. We are all friends here together. Return to your homes in peace.'

Narcisso Pinzon's head emerged from the crowd. He broadly smiled and called something in English which Leonard only heard part of. 'I...I never misjudge a man, Doctor. I tell you something: You are a great hero today...'

Leonard smiled, waved, and the crowd broke into a shatteringly loud cheer. Eloise was a little breathless as they stepped inside. 'You are indeed a great hero today,' she said, eyes sparkling.

He took her across to the office and walked in without knocking. Lieutenant Elizondo was gone but Colonel Ortez and General Miranda, drinking more coffee, arose and smiled. With Ortez that smile did not come easily, but obviously he was a soldier not a diplomat. Still, he very gallantly got a chair for Eloise and went to the door to send one of the nurses for more coffee. It was typical of the military—and not just in Columbia—that when they entered the building of someone else they habitually acted as though they owned it.

General Miranda, curious about that great cheer, asked what it had meant. Leonard explained without mentioning any of the threats. One did not necessarily have to be a diplomat to realize that threats to destroy airfields, roads, and plans to erect new hospitals, were not the best of all methods to influence the military.

Miranda was thoughtful. 'I don't believe any of the other foreign medical teams have won that much acclaim, Doctor. And incidentally, Mr Lleras told us a short while ago that it was you who swung Jorge Ritter Avila round on the land reform program. I think, since his brother-in-law the President was in a quandary over what to do in *Señor* Avila's case, that you may now also become a hero to the President. You have definitely removed him from a very prickly situation.'

The coffee came. They had a moment to pass it around. The nurse who brought it inquired of Eloise if there was anything else she could bring. Eloise would have gone out into the reception room, nearly full now of ailing—and curious—people, but General Miranda detained her with a quiet question.

'*Señorita,* this wedding really should be held in

Bogotá where people know how to celebrate a good union. These *campesinos...*' Miranda lifted broad shoulders and dropped them, looking apologetically at Eloise.

She understood his delicate non-comment and smiled back. 'But they are our friends, General. One should have one's friends at a wedding, shouldn't one?'

Miranda bent his head, saying no more. Colonel Ortez looked with frank longing after Eloise when she departed, then, seeing Leonard's gaze upon him, suddenly became very busy with his cup of coffee.

Miranda said, 'Lieutenant Elizondo has so much to learn, Doctor. But we were all young once and full of enthusiasm, weren't we?'

Leonard politely nodded, but his private reservations included some less charitable thoughts about someone 'learning' while being permitted to carry loaded pistols about.

Colonel Ortez, obviously a taciturn, direct officer, said that Lieutenant Elizondo would be reassigned when they got back to Bogotá. With a look in the depths of his eyes that Leonard didn't especially like, Ortez said, 'There are *bandoleros* in the high plains country where it freezes every night, where the wind blows incessantly all day long, and where the earth is flakes of flint. It should be an excellent place for a young officer to learn judgement and forbearance.'

If cruel-eyed Olmega Ortez said it was a harsh land where they would send Honorio Elizondo, Leonard was willing to wager it was one of the harshest places on earth.

Miranda, later on, put through a telephone call to Bogotá blandly reported complete success in all avenues, including the land distribution programme, received his instructions and rang off to solemnly drop a sly wink in Leonard's direction. 'Dr, Jorge Ritter Avila sent me a note while you were out front with that crowd. You know what is in it because he made you the offer. What shall I tell the government when I get back, that you will agree to remain one more year to help establish the hospital so that the government will be spared the expenses of operating the place for one year?'

Leonard couldn't give his answer then and there. 'The offer included Nurse Cutler,' he said. 'I haven't discussed it with her yet, General. If I may have a bit more time. . .?'

'Of course,' purred the suave, handsome officer, arising and smiling. 'All the time you wish. Colonel Ortez and I have just been recalled. Could you go now and ask Miss Cutler? We will wait.'

Leonard almost laughed aloud. He was to take all the time he wished, providing it wasn't more than the very next fifteen or twenty minutes.

He left the office, waved to Narcisso who was sitting out there among the sick people, and headed straight for the ward.

Eloise was not there. One of the nurses said she thought Nurse Cutler might be in one of the examination rooms with a patient. He went there, found Eloise and also found Alfredo; he'd opened his mouth at the wrong time again. This time he only had a big purple black eye. Eloise was scolding him heartily and Alfredo was taking it in head-hung dejection.

Leonard laughed and they both looked up when he entered. Eloise smiled and Alfredo, looking sheepish, also smiled. He averted his head so Eloise could not

174

see, and winked. Leonard winked back. Obviously and despite Eloise's fierce scoldings, Alfredo Pinzon was going to be a chronic patient. The best thing they could do was grin and bear it.

Chapter Twenty One

There was a quiet stir throughout the hospital as though each patient had some interest in local events. Whether they actually *had* an interest or not, like free people everywhere they were full of opinions and advice. Since they could not for varying reasons arise and go forth to join the mob in the plaza, they harangued one another.

Of course news of Leonard's proposal to Eloise was common knowledge after an hour or so. That also came under discussion. Some, with feelings of lingering resentment against Eloise, said Dr Bordon could do much better; that Nurse Cutler did not have a good disposition, nor was she possessed of the common touch.

There were a few—nearly all women—who said Nurse Cutler was too good for *any* man, but if she felt some great compulsion to marry, then at least she could have done much worse than Dr Bordon. Of course both factions were simply applying their own private sentiments about men and women in general to this particular impending union.

But there was one thing upon which all the people were in thorough agreement. Lieutenant Honorio Elizondo should be shot. It was natural, normal, even mandatory. They were outraged when Alfredo—who got it from Narcisso—told them Elizondo was not even to be stripped of his rank.

Fortunately these people were bedridden or there might have been another petition circulated, another mob formed.

Colonel Ortez took Elizondo up the plaza to the barracks. There, since the soldiers themselves never mentioned what ensued, it could only be guessed at. But Leonard, who'd had plenty of time to appraise Ortez, had few illusions. Afterwards too, the soldiers appeared less slovenly, more alert; it was, Leonard thought, indicative of the sharp tongue of Olmega Ortez. Later, Colonel Ortez implemented a suggestion Leonard made to General Miranda: He released the alleged *bandoleros* from the jailhouse so that they too could participate in the land reform.

But before that, he took Eloise out back of the dispensary where cool shadows showed that the morning was gone, that afternoon was coming in, low and golden over Magdalena Valley. There were still trees and distant sounds of life all around. He told her of Miranda's request and the length of time they were allotted to make their decision.

She wasn't downcast, as he'd had half expected, nor even very reluctant, but she said, 'I suppose if we don't agree to stay the hospital will turn into just another dispensary.'

He thought that very probable.

'And the staff. Does Mr Avila have any idea what it will cost to import a pathologist and retain him for a full year, not to mention interns, registered nurses, anesthesiologists, diagnosticians?'

Leonard stated that he hadn't discussed any of this with Avila, but he also said, since Jorge Avila was far from dense, or insular in his views and comprehensions, he must have had some idea of the cost before he'd made the offer.

'But it doesn't ring quite true, Leonard. He's an arch-conservative. Look how he nearly precipitated a war over that worthless land. Why should he do such a total about-face?'

Leonard smiled. 'The Latin temperament, love. When these people hate, they hate with every fibre of their being. They love the same way. Jorge Avila made his about-face grudgingly, but when he finally made it, he did not hold back at all.'

'Do you trust him?'

Leonard nodded because he knew how alike he and Jorge Avila were despite such totally different backgrounds and native environments. 'I trust him.'

'And—will you stay for another year?'

'Yes.'

She took his hand, led him back to a small bench and sat down. 'Then I will too.'

'But you mustn't do it reluctantly, Eloise. You mustn't feel you have to stay because I've said I'll stay.' He sat beside her. 'If you want to leave I'll also leave.'

'And the hospital. . .?'

He looked at her hair, at her heavy, full lips at the soft-glowing eyes she lifted to his face. 'They can find others just as competent.'

She shook her head. 'As competent, no doubt, but as experienced?'

One of the little nurses came, looking self-conscious at locating them together in their privacy. Apologetically she said the mayor was seeking them Leonard said to send him on out to them. Moments later, when Elfego Sanchez appeared, he looked anxious.

'There is a rumour,' he blurted out, 'that you two

178

will be leaving Puna with the general.'

Leonard looked at Eloise. Here was another force at work demanding a decision. She said, speaking slowly and quietly, 'No, Mr Sanchez, we won't be leaving. Mr Avila has agreed to support the new hospital for a year if we'll stay to supervise it. We'll stay, of course.'

Sanchez's worried exprssion was instantly replaced with a broad smile. He seemed greatly relieved. 'I will tell my wife,' he said. 'She was upset about that rumour.'

Eloise asked if he'd been round to see his daughter. He had, and his Elena was looking extremely well. She had smiled and joked a little, he told them, and that girl Felicidad with whom she was in company, there too was an example of the wisdom of Doctor Bordon. Felicidad, one of Sanchez's great worries, was clean and wholesome again, with a purpose. She was nursing Elena.

There were a dozen other things Elfego Sanchez told them, each in some way related to the professional skills of either Eloise or Leonard, which had in many ways uplifted the soul of the Indian-mestizo community.

'And now I must hurry back to Mister Lleras,' he finally said, preparing to depart. 'The people who have registered for their allotment of land are impatient to get to work.'

They arose to follow Sachez back into the building. Eloise touched Leonard and when he turned she threw both arms around his neck. He held her close. It was a warm, compassionate embrace and kiss. Afterwards, still holding him, she said it was a miracle that a man with his talents had arrived when he had because he hadn't just touched the lives, the hopes and spirits of the natives, he'd also made his impression upon her own outlooks and viewpoints as well.

179

They went inside and saw General Miranda in conversation with Mayor Sanchez. Elfego departed as they walked forward. Miranda, glancing up from his watch, 'I have ordered my aircraft delayed,' he informed them. 'The mayor will send word to the pilot.'

Leonard, who'd got the impression earlier that Miranda was in haste to leave Puna, mildly wondered. But he was discreet and asked no questions. Instead he told Miranda he and Eloise had agreed to stay one more year.

Miranda was pleased, genuinely so, and said they must then go tell *Don* Jorge. The reception room where they were standing was bustling with activity. Eloise's two native nurses were very professionally making their initial examinations of the dozens of people filling the large room. As Miranda, Eloise and Leonard turned to enter the ward one of the nurses came over to ask if it would be all right to release Alfredo Pinzon; she said Alfredo's black eye was hardly serious enough to keep him in the dispensary, and he was going round talking with other patients, disrupting the routine. Eloise glanced round. So did Leonard. She was seeking Alfredo but Leonard was looking for Narcisso. He found him and beckoned.

Narcisso's black eyes were amiable as he strolled over, removing his hat. Before Leonard could speak Narcisso said, 'I understand, Doctor. I will find him and take him away.'

'Far away, Narcisso,' suggested Leonard. 'Back to the *estancia* and this time see that he stays there. Otherwise I'm going to ask Mayor Sanchez to jail him.'

Narcisso nodded but made no immediate move to depart. He said, 'Doctor; Father Eusebio wants a word with you at the church when you can spare the time.'

Leonard nodded and turned to join Miranda and Eloise at the door of the ward.

Jorge Avila was watching the commotion in the ward with alert interest. It seemed he'd never before been hospitalized in his life; the experience was both novel and interesting. When they stopped beside his bed Avila pointed to an old man down the ward and getting into one of the iron cots across the room.

'That is Ernesto Velarde; he was one of our men twenty years ago when I was just learning the ropes. I've often wondered whatever became of him.'

General Miranda glanced without much interest at the old man being helped into bed. Leonard also looked but he had never before seen the old man therefore his presence was only of mild professional interest.

Avila looked up at them, his gaze pensive. 'It might be a good idea for everyone to come here once a year or so and see these people.'

Eloise bent to straighten the covers over Avila's mighty shoulders. 'Not everyone,' she quietly told him. 'But it wouldn't hurt if the landowners came, Mister Avila. The other people, the *campesinos*, already know what we do here.'

Avila's gold-flecked eyes went up to her face with a wistful look in their depths. 'I have been lying here thinking. It came to me that any decision a man makes, if he doesn't change it often, very soon becomes a wrong decision. I'm not apologizing for my resistance to meddling foreigners in Magdalena Valley. I'm only saying I've changed my decision a little.'

She smiled at him. 'Of course, *Don* Jorge.'

'You are laughing at me,' he accused.

'No. I am just beginning to understand you,' she told him.

181

'And you will stay one more year?'

She straightened up. 'Doctor Bordon and I will both stay.'

Avila looked at Leonard. 'We will remain enemies,' he exclaimed. General Miranda looked uneasy but Leonard merely nodded.

'Of course, Mister Avila. I would have it no other way. We shall remain enemies until you decide it is no longer necessary.'

Avila's long-lipped mouth loosened. He also smiled but not quite. 'General; you will stay for their wedding?'

A shadow passed across Miranda's face so fleetingly it was hard to say it had ever been there. 'Of course,' he said.

Leonard came to Miranda's rescue. 'It's really not necessary, General. You'll have things awaiting your presence in Bogatá.'

But Miranda, the diplomat, had no intention of going contrary to the wishes of the brother-in-law of the President of the Republic. He smiled and pushed out both hands, palms downward. 'Nothing so important it could prevent me from witnessing this marriage. But I wonder—how can *Don* Jorge in his present condition, be escorted to the church? Wouldn't that be very dangerous?'

Leonard conceded that it would. Eloise had the answer for them. 'We will be married right here, at his bedside.'

Avila's eyes brightened and General Miranda nodded stoically. It was settled. The three of them left Avila and returned to the front office. There, they found Father Lopez pacing the floor in obvious impatience. They explained where the wedding was to be held and Father Lopez, by nature, a non-conformist himself, did not argue. In fact he seemed pleased—or perhaps, as Leonard shrewdly guessed, he was relieved; by now Father Lopez'd had his second thoughts about marrying people who might not be catholics, in his orthodox catherdral.

One of the little nurses came to plead for Eloise's help. She left with the woman. General Miranda suggested that he and Father Lopez take Leonard to the hotel for breakfast. Until that moment Leonard had quite forgot that he hadn't had a bite to eat since long before the arrival of the helicopter bearing Miranda and Ortez.

They left the dispensary by a rear door in order to avoid the patient crowd out front in the piazza, but, as Father Lopez pointed out, they could not avoid the mob indefinitely.

'My people are very persistent, very patient. They will sit down out there and wait all day, all night, and all day tomorrow, until you go tell them you mean to stay, Doctor. And after that—of course they will want a celebration.'

General Miranda listened, then nodded agreement. 'I know how these country people celebrate, Doctor, so I would advise that you eat a large breakfast—drink lots of milk. You will be expected to drink with every man out there. You must prove your manhood. The only way to do that and not pass out is to line your insides with much milk. I'll show you how it's done at breakfast.'

183

Chapter Twenty Two

Father Lopez and General Miranda had overlooked something. Although Leonard was *simpatico*—was in sympathy with the *campesinos*—he was still his own man. He had no intention of passing out nor of drinking with everyone in that plaza. In fact he had no intention of being part of any day-long and night-long celebration for the elemental reason, as he explained to Miranda and Father Lopez, that he saw nothing much to celebrate.

Don Jorge Avila was not going to die, Elena Sanchez was reasonably whole again, the patients he and Eloise had cured and cared for were back among their friends and families, but none of this was the result of miracles.

'These are the things medical practioners and dispensaries are trained to facilitate. There's nothing at all to celebrate. In any city in the world these things are accomplished every day of the week and——'

'Doctor,' said suave General Francisco Miranda with an ironic twinkle in his eyes. 'this is Puna in the Magdalena Valley where in a thousand years there has never been a real dispensary nor hospital. Imagine how it must have been in ancient Britain when the first few fatal illnesses were cured by physicians. There were celebrations. You must not disappoint the people.'

Father Lopez, when Leonard gazed his way, merely

184

shrugged. He could not condone a drunken orgy, yet on the other hand he was humanist and realist enough to realize that what the General had just said was the literal truth. He ordered two more large glasses of half milk, half cream, for Leonard.

They were returning to the dispensary when Colonel Ortez stepped forth from the barracks and smartly saluted, smiling. He was, obviously, back in his proper element. They paused a moment to talk, then moved on. The people in the plaza began to stir, to come to life as word passed round Doctor Bordon was coming. Father Lopez noticed it first, and sighed, He had no comment to make.

Narcisso Pinzon came forth. He had sent his brother back to the *estancia* in the company of two stalwart mestizos from Puna. He assured Leonard there would be no additional problems with Alfredo. Then he held up a smudged bottle.

Leonard reluctantly drank one small swallow. General Miranda did likewise and Father Lopez looked stonily at Narcisso, who indulgently smiled, saying, 'Well, Little Father, there is a time for the rejoicing of the soul and a time for the rejoicing of the belly.' He said this in soft Spanish, but they all understood it.

Other men came forward, grinning, calling quietly for Doctor Bordon to drink with them. Most had already been at it. Leonard displayed a shrewd cameraderie; he put an arm around a shoulder here and there, gripped an extended hand, joked with some, laughed with others, all the while easing forward through the crowd towards the doors of the dispensary. He felt like a politician running for office. He could never afterwards say he hadn't felt mellow and honoured, but he did manage to avoid most of the bottles. At the door when a powerful, large young man standing impassively with old Raymondo Reyes—who proved to be one of the old man's stalwart sons—pressed a tiny gold crucifix into his hand, Leonard stopped, looked at the donor and said in Spanish, 'It is good to see there are some who know where to place the *real* homage.'

Old Raymondo gravely nodded, His powerful son smiled gently. A bond was sealed then and there amid the noise and dust and hum of sounds, then Leonard went into the dispensary where Eloise was giving instructions to one of her native nurses. She saw him at once. He went over to ask if she was prepared to be married. She said hardly; that she didn't want to be married in a white uniform. But if he would wait in the office she'd go and change. He bent over and whispered.

'Make it fast; there's enough whiskey out there to float a battleship. I'm going to have to drink some of it but I don't want to start until after the ceremony.'

She smiled. 'You won't have to drink any of it if you don't wish to, love,' and swiftly turned to leave. He had no idea what she'd meant but people were crowding inside so he made no move to detain her and went directly to his office. Father Lopez and General Miranda were right behind him. There was a third man elbowing his way anxiously forward too. He was nearly barred from the office by General Miranda, but Leonard, seeing who it was, called over for Ed Lleras to be admitted.

Lleras was dark with perspiration, his face was shiny and his eyes glowed. He had some wilted papers in one hand. With these held aloft he said, 'The first parcels of land have been filed upon and deeds given, Doctor.

You have done something for these people they should never forget.'

Leonard waved that kind of talk away. 'Ed; all I've done was exactly what I'm supposed to do; patch up people. There's no need at all to honour me for simply doing my job. I don't want to hear you say I'm responsible again. You and your government should get the acclaim.' He grinned. 'You should also have to drink the damned whiskey.'

Lleras knew his people better than Leonard suspected. He said, 'Doctor; every village in Latin America has one *patron* it always honours on a particular day. Today you can see how this tradition begins. Each year from now on, on this same day, they will celebrate your memory. It's unusual though; ordinarily the *patron* is some soldier. I think it's significant that Puna will honour a man who saves lives, instead of takes them.'

General Miranda made a thin little wry smile and went to gaze out the window. Fortunately he'd already demonstrated himself to be more diplomat than soldier.

Leonard asked Lleras to go get Narcisso Pinzon and bring him to the office. He didn't explain why and Ed Lleras didn't inquire. He simply departed to do as requested.

Father Lopez had his Bible but significantly he did not have his orthodox shawl; no priest could marry non-catholics wearing that sacred garment. Otherwise though Father Lopez gave no indication that he was aware he was marrying protestants.

They heard a low, trilling whistle out beyond the door. Leonard did not understand what it meant but both the priest and general knew. Miranda turned, hands clasped behind his back, a little gentle smile upon his handsome features. Father Lopez reached to open the door.

Eloise stood there just for a moment before stepping into the room. She was wearing a light tan suit with a sheer white blouse beneath the jacket. She wore only one bit of jewellery, a gold necklace with a tiny cross lying against her creamy throat. Her face was softly radiant and she saw no one in the room but Leonard.

She didn't look like Nurse Cutler at all. In fact she looked like a girl instead of a woman of nearly twenty-one years. Leonard felt his throat constrict. She was very lovely, very round and full and flawless in his eyes. General Miranda was perhaps the only man in the room who could have done justice in words to her beauty, and he remained silent, looking, admiring, but saying nothing.

Father Lopez closed the door after her. Outside, that soft, trilling whistle died and a long silence ensued. Evidently Father Lopez, embarrassed by the whistling, felt an explanation was necessary.

'It is not meant to be disrespectful,' he said of the trilling low whistle. 'It is their way of showing appreciation. In another tone they whistle to show derision, but this was the sound of respect and admiration. It is an ancient custom. I hope you will understand.'

Eloise turned to smile at Father Lopez. 'I should thank them,' she said, alleviating the priest's embarrassment, then she walked over to Leonard and held forth her fisted left hand. He looked enquiringly but placed his own hand palm-up. She dropped a smooth, heavy golden wedding band upon his palm.

'My mother's ring,' she said. 'Her mother's ring before that. Do you object?'

He didn't object. In fact he couldn't have objected

in any case because he had no substitute.

General Miranda finally spoke. 'I suppose the ward could be cleared out. . . .'

Leonard shook his head. 'Too many of those people have been waiting all morning, General. They deserve to watch.'

Father Lopez opened the door. He and General Miranda left first. As Leonard and Eloise walked forth the crowding people made that same bizarre low, trilling sound again.

Ed Lleras sweatily pushed through holding tightly to Narcisso Pinzon's sleeve. No one made any attempt to stop them. In fact, as they moved ahead, so did the crowd of attentive smiling people.

At the ward doorway Eloise's two little sturdy native nurses came forth to stop the crowd. Leonard leaned down.

'They want to witness it,' he said. 'I think they should, don't you?'

At once the nurses stepped aside.

Jorge Avila saw them coming. He was flat on his back but his head rolled on the pillow. He smiled and moved one clenched hand. There were two envelopes in it. Father Lopez stopped beside the bed, uncertain, waiting for Avila to speak. Back to the wide-open doors the crowd halted, people spilling round the front rank among the beds. Voices swelled in a sighing whisper as people spoke aside to one another, to the patients in bed, to the pair of little nurses.

Avila was smiling. 'Take the envelopes,' he said to the priest. 'One for *him*, one for *her*.'

Father Lopez obeyed. There was nothing written on either envelope so presumably whatever was inside was identical in both cases. He handed an envelope to Eloise

189

another envelope to Leonard.

Avila said, 'You are not yet married so until you are the envelopes are not to be opened.' He looked long at Eloise. 'A man oftentimes thinks how it would be if he ever found the perfect woman for him.' The tawny eyes were soft. 'In a man's dreams no other man could ever supersede him. In life that isn't so. Well; it wouldn't have worked anyway. We belong to different worlds. Still, a man never stops wondering.

Eloise bent far over, kissed Avila on the cheek and straightened back. 'Keep on thinking about it,' she murmured. 'Your turn will come, I know it will.'

Leonard reached down to grip the huge man's limp hand. Avila weakly squeezed back. 'Still enemies,' he muttered, his gold-flecked eyes something absolutely contrary to his words. 'Well, Doctor; where is the ring?'

Leonard placed it in Avila's hand.

Father Lopez began the simple movements which would precede his reading of the marriage ceremony. When all was in readiness he raised his close-cropped head. The ward was totally silent. Narcisso Pinzon was standing directly behind Leonard. He looked out, winked at the priest and nodded his head. Father Lopez's lips lifted slightly in a soft-faint little smile. He began reading.

It was a short ceremony. When it was over and the ring had been slipped into place Leonard looked into the faces of the people around him. General Miranda was thoughtful. Father Lopez was enormously relieved. Narcisso Pinzon broadly smiled and Elfego Sanchez dabbed at one eye with a limp handkerchief.

Ed Lleras's shirt was darker than ever. There was a muffled sniffle or two from among the women patients and an old man chuckled deep-down.

190

Jorge Avila said, 'Now open the envelopes.'

In each envelope was a cheque drawn upon the major Columbian bank in Bogata. In both cases the amount was exactly right for one year's salary.

Avila said, 'You see; it's no present at all. It's simply your pay for one year more. When you cash those cheques you will have to stay.'

Eloise smiled through a little mist and Leonard said, '*Don* Jorge, we'd have stayed anyway. We couldn't possibly have left so many friends—and enemies.'

The people back by the door began their low-humming conversation again. Several surreptitiously produced bottles but the little native nurses turned, stern and unrelenting, to make the crowd move back out into the reception room.

General Miranda leaned to whisper into Leonard's ear. 'And now, Doctor, you must go out there and accept their liquid humour. I wish you well.'

Eloise faced her husband. He sighed. 'I'd rather just go up into the mountains for a few days.' She nodded through that little mist.

'Later, my love. And I'll be waiting with the bromo-seltzer when you can get away.'

He leaned and kissed her. That brought the same trilling whistle again. Everyone loudly laughed and spoke at once. The solemn mood was broken, the mood of celebration was beginning.